TYRANT LIZARD™
AND OTHER SCIENCE-FICTION TALES

TYRANT LIZARD™
AND OTHER SCIENCE-FICTION TALES

by

Julian Michael Carver

A COLLECTION OF SHORT STORIES AND FLASH FICTION

OTHER BOOKS BY
JULIAN MICHAEL CARVER

THE TRIASSIC SERIES

Triassic
Triassic 2: Revenant
Primal Target: A Triassic Story

THE MEGACROC SERIES

Megacroc
Megacroc: Origins

STANDALONE NOVELS

Freshwater: The Adapted Movie Novelization

Pteranodon Press

Tyrant Lizard and Other Science-Fiction Tales / Julian Michael Carver

ISBN: 979-8-9877526-2-3

14 13 12 11 10 / 10 9 8 7 6 5 4 3 2 1

After you've read this book, please consider learning an honest review of the book online.

Reviews help authors get noticed.

Thank you.

Julian Michael Carver

Dedicated to Shar-Kel and the Shar-Kel editing service.

Thanks for reading my stories and providing feedback necessary to bring this collection to life!

I couldn't have done this without you and your editorial team.

- J.M.C.

TABLE OF CONTENTS

AUTHOR'S PREFACE

Tyrant Lizard and Other Science-Fiction Tales is my first self-published short story and flash fiction collection. This may come as a surprise to readers familiar with my work, but this book isn't a dinosaur-only collection. Numerous sub-genres are explored, including hard science fiction, military science-fiction, space opera, cyberpunk, time-travel, and artificial intelligence. For this collection, I didn't want to feel tied down with a rigid theme, but rather have the freedom to write a variety of stories.

I like to think there's something for everyone in this book. Some old-school sci-fi readers might like the harder themes of *Bioluminescense* or *Transference*, but millennials might enjoy colorful tales like *Cat-Like Reflexes*. I even stayed true to my origins with creature-features for my Severed Press audience; *Death Dive*, *Tooth and Claw* and, of course, *Tyrant Lizard*.

Ideally, I'd love to release one science-fiction collection per year, but that might be difficult with my annual commitment of one novel and kid's book—but we'll see!

Right now, enjoy my first short story collection of which I'm very proud.

THE TEMPLE GUARDIAN

BY

JULIAN MICHAEL CARVER

"Keep moving, dickhead, before I convert your head to gray matter!"

Poncho Clement complied, keeping his head down while trying not to irritate the burly man two steps behind him. Not that Poncho couldn't handle the thug, Sara thought. She had seen her companion take down numerous mercenaries over the course of their adventure. But now Poncho was unarmed, while his captor brandished a sawed-off needle-gun, leveling the barrel to the back of his neck.

A second barrel nudged her neck, sending an icy wave jolting through her body.

"I like the way your knees shake", came the creepy voice behind her.

She ignored the perverted comment, but ignoring the chilling touch of a needle-gun was no easy task.

She cringed, curling her fingers in fright while prodded along the dark passage.

"Just do what they say," Poncho whispered, peering over to her. "Maybe they'll let us go."

Don't count on it, Sara thought to herself, managing a nod. She knew panicking wouldn't help; in fact, it might even instigate the grave robbers.

Poncho was used to dealing with cutthroat treasure-hunters. He had been in laser-fights on Saturn XV, survived star-shuttle chases from Eris I, and even braved the Kuiper Asteroid Field on multiple occasions. Rumor had it, he even survived a near encounter with a lunar venom crawler.

Yet despite all these extraordinary feats, Sara knew their odds of surviving the current predicament weren't very high.

Two men with needle-guns marched behind them. Needle-weaponry was a deadly new innovation in the past century. The technology fired crystalline shards from a piston-powered electrode accelerator. Even a single needle shard to the shoulder could effectively dispatch an opponent.

Ahead, the gang's fearsome enforcer, whom Poncho recognized as Captain Viper Soten, a notorious space pirate, proceeded down the ancient corridor with a flashlight. He was draped in a Union admiral's frock coat; a foe whom Viper undoubtedly killed. Sara ascertained he wasn't to be trifled with. At his belt, the pirate brandished a rapier blade with a golden hilt made to resemble a wyvern. On the opposite side of the belt hung a needle-flintlock pistol, one of the earlier models of needle military tech. flintlocks, Sara presumed, were manufactured more for their attractive antique feel than their practicality in combat. Nonetheless, even a single-shot needle flintlock was a deadly firearm.

A few steps to the front of the Captain walked a scout whom Viper referred to as 'Ramirez'. Ramirez moved cautiously, feeling the granite blocks along the walls for hidden dart launchers.

"Step lightly," Ramirez called out, shining the flashlight taped to his needle-gun across the tiled floor. "Looks like another 'hop-scotch' trap."

His flashlight illuminated a cubic pattern stenciled into the floor. Several cubes formed a mosaic sidewalk. A prior trap through the maze confirmed the green squares were the correct areas that accepted human foot traffic. The remaining colors—blue, red and yellow were pressurized triggers for snare guns hidden in the walls, installed over a millennia ago. The temple was constructed with elegant statues and masterful paintings, but also boasted an array of hidden armament.

Sara stepped delicately along the green squares when it was her turn to pass. Halfway across the primitive pattern, she froze. To her terror, her right shoe was touching a red tile. Red polygons triggered darts from both sides of the walls; an unavoidable death sentence administered instantaneously. They learned this at the cost of Viper's original lead scout, Taylor, who quickly succumbed to the deadly neurotoxins contained within the multiple projectiles. Ramirez was promptly promoted, although not willingly, to lead scout.

"Why don't you just let us go?" Poncho called defiantly to Viper, a muscular pirate who looked the part. "You've already found the lunar temple of Seirios. You *really* think we're of any use now that you know all the traps?"

"Quite the contrary, Mr. Clement," the pirate turned, bearing a sinister grin behind his shoulder-length dark hair. "I need Ms. Breslin here to decipher any of the Zharda inscriptions and hieroglyphics on the walls. We've already got lost twice because none of us can read Zharda inscriptions. I'm happy we commandeered you when we did. Otherwise, we'd be stuck in here for hours looking for the sarcophagus chamber."

"What about him?" Sara nodded to Poncho. "Let him go, if you just need me."

"He's still useful," Viper replied. "I may yet need another scout. The Zharda built these temples with death in mind for all trespassers. We may encounter more traps that we aren't anticipating."

Viper was right, although Sara hated to admit it. Fifteen hundred years ago, when Earth's colonization efforts were in their infancy, the Zharda colonized the planet Terra IX. Once settled, they built temples and cities in honor of their deity, the star god known as Seirios. The Zharda culture flourished on Terra IX for a millennia, until a meteor shower rendered a planet-wide extinction.

The destruction of Terra IX was a tale of legend, depicted in art and theatrical holo-film across the galaxy. With the coordinates of the planet shrouded in mystery, numerous space-farers risked their lives in search of the lost world, hoping to raid the temple of Seirios. A legend of the temple surfaced a hundred years earlier when a withered scroll washed up on the coast of Okeanos. The scroll alluded to a massive technological innovation hidden within the sarcophagus of the central Seirios temple.

Ownership of the scroll changed hands several times, either by auction or murder. Poncho Clement came into its possession after winning a star-port auction.

Translating Zharda text was difficult. Few were fluent in translating documents from the extinct race. Sara Breslin, whom happened to be at the right place at the right time, overheard some traders talking about Poncho's discovery at a spaceport. It took a year to track him down.

When they finally met, she offered to translate in exchange for a portion of the riches once the temple was found. Poncho agreed, in dire need of a translator.

The shaky partnership was spent predominately scouring spacial maps for lost planets. Somewhere along the way, the pair moved their professional efforts to a flirtatious tryst, and finally, non-stop love-making when star-travel permitted.

Was becoming the lover of a fabled treasure-hunter what Sara intended when they teamed up? Of course not, but she certainly didn't mind the result.

Space-faring got lonely, she thought. *And traveling for light-years with a legend like Poncho Clement has its perks.*

Ramirez stopped short ahead, reaching a fork in the dark tunnel. Sara watched as his flashlight danced over artful hieroglyphs, chiseled at a time unknown by a masterful Zharda artist. The craftsmanship of the colorful depictions were meticulously unique. Sara marveled at the straight lines, arcing circles, and chiseled serifs. Viper walked up beside Ramirez, cocked his neck, and spat on the stunning masterpiece.

"Time to earn your keep, sweetheart," the captain grumbled. "You're up."

He scratched one of the hieroglyphs with his rapier, rendering the ornate symbol to dust.

"It's Sara, *asshole*," she shot back, moving between the murderous pirates.

"Don't piss me off, bitch," Viper grinned, exposing gold teeth and cavity-laden molars. "Just read the damn Sanskrit and tell us which way to the sarcophagus."

Sara looked away, avoiding eye contact with the cutthroat corsair. The scrolling text on the wall was a chore to translate. Many lines eroded over time, crumbling to dust mounds that buried ornate floor trim. From prior directional markers along the way, she was able to pinpoint their location on a carved map near the center. Alternating between the legible lines, Sara gleaned the chamber supposedly housing the sarcophagus was near—possibly at the end of the next corridor.

"We're close," Sara observed, running her fingers over the ancient directional indicators. "We take the right turn here and this should open up to a wider chamber ahead. Supposedly, the sarcophagus of Seirios should be laying in the following crypt, in plain sight."

"You heard her," Viper sneered at Ramirez. "Lead the way. The rest of you, fall in behind. And Mr. Clement. Don't get cute. You try to run, and I'll kill her."

"You lay one finger on her and *I'll*—"

"It's okay, Poncho," Sara replied, pushing the two men apart. "I'll play ball—I promise."

"I like a woman who takes orders," Viper smiled, starting after Ramirez. "Keep a heads up for any booby-traps along the ground! Remember the corner-mount dart launchers too, unless you wanna end up like Derrick and Taylor."

"Aye, sir," Ramirez nodded, loathing the responsibility.

The corridor fed straight ahead. A minute later, a stairwell appeared, leading down twenty golden steps. At the base of the stairwell, the passage became increasingly grand. Gold majestic creatures beveled out from the walls, carved to resemble galactic dragons or asteroid serpents, coiling around unknown planetary systems. Majestic columns bordered the edges, ascending ten meters until they met with a glossy ceiling of flawless quartz. Her reflection was so clear, Sara wondered if they were walking below a glass aquarium.

"Keep moving!" barked one of the pirates behind her. "No time to admire. The prize ahead is far greater than gold."

"Not that we'll be around long enough to see it," Poncho muttered, promptly receiving a shove to his back.

"Cheer up, Mr. Clement," Viper snickered near the front. "I'm toying with the idea of letting you both go. Who knows? I might be in a good mood once I see what's in the sarcophagus."

"Don't flatter us, Viper," Poncho scoffed. "I've heard stories of what you've done to your captives. The hostages on Eden IV didn't need to die. You executed them in cold blood. How can you be so evil?"

"Holo-clip news media is so one-sided, isn't it," Viper shot back, following Ramirez through the columns. "Had you been there, you would've seen it was a matter of survival to do what I did. The wife was injured in a fall. Husband went mad and lunged at my teamI'm talkin' he was a complete lunatic. We *had* to kill him. The woman was a mercy killing. Of course, journalists spun the entire tale. The truth will never get out."

"You expect us to buy that yarn?" Poncho asked defiantly.

"It's your choice really," the corsair replied. "With how much you're pissing me off, your life might depend on a mere flip of a coin. Your girlfriend is pretty enough that I might allow her to live. One can't be too careful. There may be more traps on the way out that we aren't thinking of. Did you ever think, Sara, that your knowledge of Zharda might be so useful?"

"I knew it would be," Sara replied. "I just didn't know

it'd be to help the likes of *scum* like you."

"*Ouch!*" Viper said playfully. "This one's feisty. *Whoa!* What's this, Ramirez?"

"Vaulted doors of some kind, Captain, but I'm not the expert."

Viper impatiently waved Sara up, glaring over her shoulder as she surveyed the obstacle. The passage ended, culminating in two massive doors, equally as intricate as the columns and ceiling. Golden vines swirled around the pair of one-meter-tall handle bars, laden with razor-sharp chiseled thorns. Sara leaned forward and studied the handles. The doors would be impossible to open without severely injuring one's palms. Based on the interlocking design, both doors would need opened simultaneously if the sarcophagus chamber was to be accessed. Even more interesting than the vines was the strange figure embossed into the doorway. The shape, spanning both doors, resembled an Aztec painting. It was a golden being standing over eight feet tall. Its face was aglow with sunlight. Below the towering specter, hundreds of little golden people knelt before it, entranced by its beauty—or deadly power.

A deity of some sort? Sara decided, touching the ominous engraving.

"Enough gawkin'!" Viper yelled, his shout echoing through the chamber. "Open the damn thing! This *has* to be it."

"You see those thorns?" Sara pointed. "Some ancient craftsman spent significant time chiseling them into daggers. They need broken off before we can open the handles."

"Easy," the corsair chuckled. "Who's got a chisel? Rodney! Get up here and wither this shit down."

"Aye, sir."

Rodney, the large enforcer who had been standing behind Sara, shuffled forward with a hammer and chisel. Puffing a fat cigar, he set the tools in place. Then, readying his posture, he began hammering into the tangled thorns. Sara looked away, refusing to stare at the pirate defaming the historic architecture.

When she looked back, Rodney was out of breath, muscles bulging through his sweaty shirt. He wiped his brow, amazed that the thorns remained intact.

"I didn't even make a dent!" he exclaimed, examining the handles. "Viper, this gold must be blended with a protective sealant to make it more durable. They're coated with somethin'. Whatever it is, the Zharda wanted these doors sealed—permanently."

"*Preposterous!*" Viper snapped at Ramirez. "You try!"

"Aye, sir," Ramirez replied scornfully, taking the tools from Rodney.

Twenty strokes in, Sara knew the thorns would hold. As dumb as the pirates were, she knew Rodney's assessment of the handles was correct. The Zharda coated the golden thorns with a substance thick enough to ensure the archway would remain sealed. With the discovery of the impassable entrance, it all but confirmed the sarcophagus was inside, presumably undefined.

"It ain't happenin' boss," Ramirez said, fighting to catch his breath. "Too bad we didn't buy any detonators."

"What about a blast from the needle-gun?" suggested the guard behind Poncho.

"Nice one, Morrison," Rodney fired back. "Needles spread and ricochet. One burst and we'd all be dead."

"How do you intend on getting through then, dick-head?"

"Boys, boys, *boys!*" Viper snapped, grinning proudly. "See? This is why I'm in charge; for situations like this. I told you, I always have a solution. And normally, it's a very simple one. *Ready?* Here it is. We have *two* handles. We have *two* hostages. One hostage per handle. They sacrifice *their* hands for the good of *our* mission. See how this hostage-captor thing works?"

The pirates chuckled, stepping away from the pair of hostages. Ramirez and Rodney mischievously parted ways at the door, gesturing to the handles. Poncho glanced remorsefully at Sara as they approached the thorns.

"I'm sorry I got you into this," Poncho frowned, placing both palms around the handle before clenching down.

"You didn't," Sara said. "Don't apologize. I'm the one that sought *you* out. I knew we'd find the temple, Poncho. I just thought it'd be under different circumstances."

"You two love birds done?" Viper barked.

The corsairs formed a line ten feet behind, flashlights illuminating the sinister Aztec war-god.

"You've got doors to open, and we've got a tomb to raid!"

Sara swallowed, wrapping her palms delicately around the handle. She could feel their gentle sting before grabbing down, teasing her flesh at several points. She watched Poncho readying his own stance on the other side, gritting his teeth as he experimented with his grip. It would take monumental strength to open both doors; a herculean effort that promised incomprehensible anguish.

Sara grimaced, fearing both her hands would likely become disfigured. The doors looked to weigh a ton each. If either of them failed and had to retry, she feared the blood-loss might kill her.

"*Do it!*" Viper demanded impatiently, cocking the antique needle flintlock at his belt.

"Fast, okay," Poncho nodded. "Quick, hard, and *fast!*"

"Right," Sara replied, bracing herself. She gritted her teeth, imagining the pain she was about to inflict on herself. "*NOW!*"

Thorns met palms as Sara and Poncho grabbed down, pulled, cried, and bled together. Sara's teeth bit down on her lip, while tears slipped over her cheeks seconds after squeezing down. Shock waves of pain rolled up her hands, pulsating through her wrist and forearms like concentric circles in a pond. Blood rolled underneath her hands, while the thorns locked her palms at their starting positions. She could feel every muscle of her body aching as her knees quivered, fighting the jabs and the immense weight simultaneously. She coped with a loud wail, accompanied by short sobs and fatigued breaths.

For a split-second, one of her hands fell off, momentarily relieving her anguish. She was forced to grab back on a different spot, crying while the thorns found fresh places to puncture, summoning more wounds.

On the opposite end, Poncho remained mostly quiet, barring his teeth like a rabid hyena amid a consistent grunt. Most of his fingers managed to find grooves to avoid lacerations, although his palms seeped blood like a small fountain.

Through their combined efforts, both doors slowly began to budge, sliding inch by inch away from the interlocking puzzle that zig-zagged between both panels. Sara fought hard to ignore the pain. Her left hand was holding steady compared to her dominant right hand; now a mangled mess of gashes.

To her horror, she felt her energy begin to drain. Her feet skidded as the weight of the door overpowered her. Toiling hard to bring her door up to Poncho's position, Sara fought hard. She knew if it returned to the default position it might reset both their efforts.

"I'm slipping!" she cried.

"Pull!" Poncho cried, grinding his teeth. "Pull harder, Sara!"

"Ramirez, Rodney!" Viper snapped. "Get in there and help! We can't risk their hands falling apart and the doors retracting."

"*Awh*, but *Captain*—"

"Get in there or I'll kill you myself!" Viper demanded, pushing both men forward while he and Morrison watched.

"Move, bitch!" Rodney grumbled, bracing around Sara as Ramirez took a stand behind Poncho.

As Rodney began to pull, Sara felt part of her door's weight diminish. With two extra hands pulling with her, Sara doubled her efforts, ignoring the blood dripping from Rodney's hand inches above.

Across the threshold, Poncho and Ramirez quickly pulled their door ahead. Ten seconds later, their door crossed a seam in the floor. From the ceiling, a bronze bar slid down, piercing the hinges of Poncho's door and locking it into place. Ramirez hopped away, yelping in pain as he raced for a roll of gauze that Morrison was holding. Poncho spun back to help Sara and Rodney, gripping the handle with one hand near the lower edge. With three bodies at work, they clinked the second door into place five seconds after. When a second bronze rivet slammed down, Sara knew their strife had ended.

"Shit, that burns!" Rodney cussed.

The pirate fell sluggishly away as he ripped a sleeve to shreds, wrapping the tattered cloth around both palms.

Sara fell on her backside, staring in horror at both palms. Her left wasn't terrible; three thorns found their way into the center while a fourth punctured her index finger at the medial phalanges. The worse hand—the right—was an eviscerated hunk of flesh, riddled with lacerations from the insidious contraption.

Poncho wrapped his hands before turning to help Sara. Seconds after he finished, Morrison yanked them both upright.

"Enough dawdling!" Viper yelled. "Ramirez, proceed through. We've finally made it."

"Aye, sir," replied the pirate, blood soaking through his gauze-bound hands.

Ramirez retrieved his needle-gun, holding it clumsily with his impaired palms. The pirate looked like he held it more like a newborn baby than a deadly firearm.

One by one, the convoy followed him through the archway.

"Oh my God," Sara gasped, momentarily forgetting about the pain in her hands.

They found themselves standing atop a massive raised platform; a bridge bordered on both sides by a golden rail four-feet tall. The bridge, laden with a braided pattern of brickwork, fed forward until it reached a circular precipice. At the center of the platform, three concentric steps raised upward, culminating at the top platform with a maximum radius of fifteen meters. There, a single tomb awaited, encrusted with the finest gems known in the galaxy.

Sara felt her mouth open. The tomb had to be over eight feet long.

"Watch your step," Morrison announced, glaring over the rail. "Looks steep."

Sara shot a look. The bridge fell off to a presumably endless abyss. Above, ancient lanterns dangled from the ceiling fifty meters up, eternally lit with renewable fuel. The flames did wonders to illuminate the bridge and balcony. However, their photons lost their luster fifty feet below the bridge, giving no indication of the chamber's depth.

"*Boys!*" Viper announced, removing his hat as he stared in awe at the tomb. "It's payday!"

Rodney and Ramirez screeched like banshees and shuffled down the bridge toward the platform. Viper gestured Poncho and Sara to follow, while Morrison stayed behind, faithfully guarding the only exit.

"What kind of a host would I be if I didn't at least let you see what was inside?" Viper smiled deviously under his curled mustache.

"You mean before you throw us off the ledge?" Sara said, wincing from her palms.

"Just one of you," Viper added, moving them along the bridge with the barrel of his needle flintlock. "The other I might seal inside the sarcophagus. It'd be fun hearing you suffocate before the long walk back to the ship. Unless of course I decide you still might be useful for hieroglyphs, Sara. Then maybe I'll kill you on the ride home."

"You psychopathic bastard!" Poncho fired back, ignoring the flintlock teasing his shoulders. "I swear, you better *kill* me. If not, I'm coming for you, Viper!"

"I'll add you to the list of agitators claiming the same vengeance," Viper laughed, his sadistic cackle echoing through the crypt. "Oh wait, there is *no* list. Everyone that's ever threatened me has already been dealt with. Well lads, what do we have here?"

Sara and Poncho took the three steps to the top platform. Ramirez and Rodney stood on either side of the sarcophagus, taken aback by the jewel-laden rendering on the surface plate. Beveled along the lid was the same mythical figure they found on the doorway—the large golden man. As it was before, the figure's face was aglow with gold.

"Is this Seirios?" Ramirez asked, touching the illustration's visage. "Is that what's buried here?"

"It can't be!" Rodney gasped. "Seirios is just folklore. A ghost story."

"It's not Seirios," Sara uttered, examining more hieroglyphs along the jeweled coffin. "These engravings aren't withered away. They tell the tale, at least partially. Long ago, the Zharda culture abandoned their worship of their stargod—the one we call Seirios. Apparently, their civilization experienced a technological renaissance, I'd say around eleven hundred years ago. Their innovations were primarily robotic. In the decades that followed, these robots became the deities of the Zharda. One robot in particular, whom they called Ultris, became their greatest deity. According to the hieroglyphs, Ultris means the omnipotent machine; emissary of mercy and death."

"Sounds more like a judge than a deity," Rodney stated, trying to pick out some loose diamonds from the tomb.

"Sounds like a line of bullshit," Viper remarked. "There's nothing in there but the last Zharda king of the Terra IX—whoever that was. He's probably rotting in there, buried under the purest gemstones we've ever seen. Let's crack the lid off this bastard! We can let Poncho see what's inside before he walks the plank."

The bandits cackled, removing pry-bars from their backpacks. Sara took a step forward, curious at what years of her life searching for the lost planet would now culminate to. The corsairs awkwardly slid the lid away, uttering profanities stemming from their injured palms. Inch by inch the lid skidded away, until it clattered onto the platform on the side opposite the bridge.

"Well?" Morrison called from the archway. "What the hell is it?"

"It's jewels, Morrison!" Viper exclaimed, face aglow with the light of a thousand flawless stones. "Thousands and thousands of the purest jewels you've ever seen! We're rich, boys! Start pocketing the loot into your backpacks— as much as you can carry! It might take several trips to get it all in the cargo hold."

Ramirez and Rodney began shouting happily, cramming handfuls of diamonds, emeralds, sapphires, and rubies into their tattered backpacks.

Poncho shot a discreet nod to Sara and stepped backward—only to meet the barrel of Viper's needle flintlock.

"Not so fast, Mr. Clement," Viper leered.

He gestured with the pistol at the dark abyss surrounding the platform. "I believe you have a date with destiny."

"Care to join me?" Poncho asked.

"Funny," Viper grinned, aiming the pistol at the treasure-hunter's forehead. "Now, Mr. Clement. I've let you see what's inside the tomb. Now, take your last steps off the ledge, or I'll kill both you and your little—"

"*Captain!*" Rodney cried, thrusting his hand into the tomb. "The gemstones! They're sinking into the tomb!"

"What?" Viper growled, shoving past his hostages.

The sight was both confusing and surreal. Gemstones danced and fell over one another, like water draining from a tub. Both robbers raced to collect as many of the rocks as their bloody hands could clutch. It took only a few seconds for the bulk of the gems to slip away. A grate was revealed at the tomb's floor, through which the gems perished into a dark void.

As the stones vanished, a strange silhouette began to take shape. Buried under the gems and supported by the grate lay a humanoid golden figure eight feet in height. After the final stones slipped away, the bipedal skeleton was predominately visible. Aglow from dim lantern light, the figure looked almost maniacal.

No one spoke, confused at the odd turn of events. Sara was bewildered by the strange figure.

That thing has been buried here for a millennia!

"*Ummm*, what is it?" Ramirez asked.

"A gold skeleton?" Rodney guessed, touching the figure's armored shoulder-pad.

"It's not a gold skeleton," Sara stated, staring in awe. "It's Ultris, the crowning technological achievement of the Zharda at the time of their world's collapse."

The shimmering humanoid was remarkable. Crafted with the purest gold and lined with black trim that Sara guessed was onyx, the machine was a model for the perfect robot. Three faces were fitted to a neck filled with compressors and actuators. With three heads, the robot bore six eyes with what appeared to be zoom lenses. Each arm was fitted with interlocking gears and cylinders, while the fingers were spring-loaded, enabling for flexible joints and varying articulation. The legs—what she could see of them behind the golden shin-guards—bore shock-absorbing technology for ease of mobility. She brushed away gemstones nestled on the figure's feet, discovering stabilizing mechanisms and reinforced padding for bipedal motion.

"*Unbelievable!*" Poncho gasped, clutching the edge of the tomb. "The legends of the sarcophagus are true! It held the crowning jewel of the Zharda empire. It just so happens that their greatest treasure was their own creation—their god."

"If they loved their god so much," Ramirez cut in, "Why the hell did they entrap it?"

"Does it even work?" Rodney asked, ignoring his cohort's question.

"Impossible," Viper replied. "It's been lying under a heap of gems for a thousand years. Any residual power left in this thing would have drained centuries ago."

"I wouldn't be so sure," Sara corrected. "Legends describe the Zharda as excellent builders and innovators. I wouldn't be surprised if this thing had a backup generator or was fed via circuitry—"

As Sara spoke, she caught a glimpse of motion. A gear began rotating inside the machine's rib-cage, protected behind an inner-coating of plate glass. As the one gear wound up, it nudged another, then a rotor shaft, spinning more cogwheels. Soon, the entire rib-cage was winding to life, supplying enough power for LED lights to flicker on the chest cavity.

"Well slap my ass!" Rodney gawked. "The ancient crankshaft is coming to *lif*—"

The group was so preoccupied with Ultris' enduring functionality, they failed to observe a small compartment open below the machine's shoulders. Had Rodney noticed the hidden trough, it may have saved his life.

In the blink of an eye, twenty razor-sharp flechettes—two inches in length—fired from the inconspicuous chamber, humming through the air like throwing stars. The bulk of the barrage missed Rodney's head—all but three—finding their way to his exposed jugular.

Ramirez gasped, stepping back in fear.

Rodney's body toppled backward. Now a lifeless vegetable, his corpse tumbled down the steps, saved from the abyss when striking the guard rail.

"This thing's a *death machine!*" Viper screeched, racing to prepare his flintlock. "Ramirez, open fire!"

Before anyone could fathom the stunning sequence of events, Ultris snapped to an upright sitting position.

Sara stood frozen in fear, fighting the urge to watch the ancient machine. The robot's movements were robust and rigid, yet between poses it moved with fluidity and precision, especially as it orchestrated calculated attacks. Hypnotized by Ultris' deadly grace, she slowly let go of the sarcophagus—just in time to receive a metal backhand to her head.

"*Ooo-f!*"

Her world spun as the machine knocked her away from the upper platform. The move wasn't deadly but packed enough force to knock wind from her lungs. As her vision morphed into a cyclone, she heard Poncho scream her name as she tumbled down the circular steps.

The quick *rat-tat-tat* of a needle-gun went off, followed by Viper's single flintlock blast as she regained her stance. Momentum kept her going as she backpedaled clumsily toward the abyss. She felt her waist touch the saving grace of the guard-rail, but inertia hauled her over the edge. She watched the action at the sarcophogus drift to lower frame, then she saw the torchlight glimmering high above. Finally, she saw the darkness of the endless pit ready to receive her.

No!

At the last moment, Sara's body spun. Her hands grasped the guard-rail with a reverse somersault as her feet dangled over the void. She cried helplessly as her palms bled under her bandages, making clutching the guard-rail an agonizing endeavor. She couldn't hold the rail for long.

"Hang on, Sara!" Poncho screamed from the upper platform.

She saw him race down the steps after her, away from the contested upper platform. Between gasps, she saw Ultris step out from the tomb amid bursts of needle-fire. The shards whizzed and ricocheted, miraculously missing Poncho.

The golden machine deployed hidden serrated wrist blades on both arms, reminding her of a heroic samurai. With an unpredictable spin, it swiveled around on a concealed turn-table mounted somewhere beneath the rib cage, decapitating Ramirez as he attempted to reload. Sara watched Ramirez' head and torso sever and vanish on the other side of the tomb, just as she felt Poncho's hands clasp her own.

"Hang on! I have you!"

Sara cried as he struggled to yank herself over the top. Poncho cried too, his palms bleeding as he sacrificed flesh to pull her to safety.

Grunting as his strength gave out, he hauled her over the rail. They tumbled over one another, just in time to see Utris whirl around to face Viper.

The pirate captain was dual-wielding his flintlock and Ramirez' needle-gun. The corsair screamed in defiance, sending a hailstorm of needles humming at the golden warrior. Projectiles soared in all directions, dousing the balcony in a fierce storm of shards.

"*Auugh!*" Poncho cried, taking several needles to his shoulder.

"Don't stop!" Sara urged, pulling him up by one arm. "Head for the exit!"

She tugged him upright. The pair shuffled around the sarcophagus, using Viper's last stand as a distraction while scurrying for the bridge.

With a swift slash of its wrist blade, Ultris sliced apart Viper's weaponry, delivering a swift stroke with the opposite blade, slicing open his abdomen. With a bloodcurdling cry, the pirate crumpled down the steps, landing on the foot of the bridge. Ultris continued marching, ignoring the corsair's woes as it turned toward Poncho and Sara.

"Morrison you *asshole!*" Poncho screeched, limping over the bridge.

To Sara's terror, Morrison—the last remaining pirate—found a hidden release to the chamber doors; a silvery wheel serving as a closing mechanism. Both doors began to close, relieved of the bronze shafts that previously barred their movement. Morrison smiled as he prepared to leave, turning back to marvel at the sinister invention.

That was his mistake.

From behind, Sara heard the machine's flechettes snap off again, sending a wave of singing daggers toward them.

"*Auugh!*"

One knife caught her in the shoulder. Poncho screamed, receiving one in his lower back.

The remainder of the flechettes flew between, finding their way into Morrison's skull ten feet ahead. His body slammed to the floor between both rotating panels, serving as a convenient door-stop. With a clink, the doors connected at the corpse's torso. Bones were crunched as the mechanized pressure threatened to break his body asunder.

Amid the sound of Morrison's splintering bones, Sara heard a grunt behind her. Suddenly, something seized her ankle.

"Don't leave me!"

She turned around hysterically, eyeing the hindrance.

Viper, now a mess of lacerations and sweat, circumnavigated the machine's advance. With a diving run, he grabbed her leg, his crazed glance alternating between his former hostages and the oncoming security system.

"Don't leave me behind, please!" he begged, shaking his head as if prone to epilepsy.

"Get off me, shitbag!" Sara wailed, trying to pry his clammy hands from her ankle.

Wasting no time, Poncho delivered a quick jab, breaking the corsair's teeth with balled knuckles. The pirate went down, just as Ultris approached the scuffle. Blood flowing from his nostrils, Viper spun to face the machine, protesting his demise with a series of futile sobs.

"No... *please*... No.... *NO!*"

Ultris showed no emotion for Viper's surrender. In a flash, the robot extended its right wrist-blade forward, puncturing the corsair's chest. Blood flew from the wound in spurts. Now conjoined with the machine by means of the sword, Viper was forced to stare at his killer, gurgling blood while dying in agony.

"Come on!"

The machine distracted, Poncho yanked Sara through the narrow archway, the doors still held in place by Morrison's meaty chest.

Sara turned just in time to see Ultris' blade withdrawn through reverse power. Viper fell lazily to his side, dead before hitting brickwork. Ultris continued its dreadful march toward the final two targets, walking with a single purpose—preventing the intruders' escape.

"*Run!*" Sara screeched. "Head for the ship!"

"We're wounded," Poncho shot back. "We'll never make it to the ship. Here—help me move his body! The doors will seal that *thing* inside!"

Sara complied, understanding her teammate's rationale. Together, they hauled Morrison's remains from the doorway, fighting pain from their hands.

Through the closing slit in the wall, the robot maintained its pursuit. Five meters away. Three meters away. One meter away—readying another assortment of flechettes.

The slit in the closing doors shrunk to a foot. Then five inches. Then one.

With a deactivating glow, the robot halted several feet from the threshold.

Finally, the interlocking doors met, sealing Ultris inside the chamber behind the blood-laden handles.

Sara backed away, half expecting a golden blade to

pierce through the opening. A muffled whine of gears was heard through the sealed entrance, followed by a mechanical lurch that decayed with distance.

"It's going back to the tomb," Poncho said, staring at the robot's depiction on the doors. "I guess the treasure of the Zharda was the very thing programmed to guard the crypt. The greatest and final invention of Terra IX. Ultris—guardian of the capital temple."

"They entombed it there because it was too deadly to worship in person," Sara proclaimed. "It was probably meant to be worshiped right here, in front of this shrine on the doors. The thorns served as a security protocol. Evidently, they found Ultris worthy of their praise, but too unpredictable to be appreciated in-person. That's why they placed the machine in the sarcophagus. Secure, but active."

"I wonder how many poor souls died trying to fit that robot inside the tomb?" Poncho mused.

"We can debate that on our way back to the ship," Sara said. "I'm dying to get off this rock. I've decided—Terra IX is better left undisturbed."

"I completely agree," Poncho nodded. "How's your hands?"

"Killin' me. Yours?"

"Nothing some ointment and stitches won't fix. I know you hate stitches, Sara, but you really should let me take a look. Your hands looked bad, but I think we can salvage them. Viper may have had some meds we could pillage."

"For once, I'll concede," she replied. "Once we get there, please take a look. I'll lead the way back. Mind the dagger traps. I'd hate to come so close to escape only to be knifed in the ass."

"Don't make me laugh," Poncho chuckled, turning away from the Ultris shrine. "Get us out of here—preferably in one piece."

BIOLUMINESCENCE

BY

JULIAN MICHAEL CARVER

In the bright, fluorescent lights of the Locke & Strider mechatronics laboratory, sub-floor F, a pair of metallic manipulator arms descended from their rigid startup position. Equipped with end effectors in the form of pincers, the machine's nanocomputer swerved the armature toward an assembly line. There, a line of microprocessors crawled along, gleaming with pristine brilliance as they headed toward their true purpose—installation.

The armature selected the first microchip that passed by, taking the circuit in both silvery claws. Spinning the microprocessor around with both pincers, the controller of the assembly line lowered the armature. Below, a dark oval-shaped shell paused on a second conveyor belt, ready to be bestowed with the digital spark of life.

Another set of end effector pincers slid out from secondary ports, opening a pair of half-inch steel doors on the shell's head, exposing a square beveled inset. Inches above, the microprocessor was lowered down until the first armature gently placed the chip within the opening, completing the task as it sealed the hatch. The microchip in place, both sets of arms retracted to their point of origin.

With the startup process compete, the system proceeded with the second phase—prototype initialization.

The conveyor belt deposited the black shell on a final platform, exposed to the afternoon sun through a skylight in the warehouse. There, the sun's rays charged the black shell's solar panels. Inside, voltage allotted by kinetic energy was transferred to the microchip.

Gears spun.

Carbon fiber legs clicked apart.

Wings unfolded and flapped.

A pair of camera-lens optics clicked open.

At last, the robotic insect prototype, the L&S Firefly Mk. 1, was ready for trial run.

Locke & Strider, a biological corporation invested in wildlife conservation, had numerous multi-million dollar endeavors in the works. One of their lesser known projects involved restoring the firefly population west of Kansas. The L&S Firefly Mk. 1 was developed to goad firefly migration, equipped with a small light beacon to encourage copulation. Although the project, code-named *Operation: Bioluminescence,* wasn't one of the corporation's more lucrative endeavors, the staff saw it as a passion project with an exciting prototype; a fully articulate life-size robotic firefly, fueled by the sun and programmed with adaptive learning.

Motion sensors detecting a disturbance in the shadows, the L&S Firefly Mk. 1 tilted forward, shifting weight to its abdomen. Solar power converting to binary data within the robot's nanocomputer, the Firefly Mk.1 spread its wings wide. Moving faster than an industrial fan at a rate of 250 RPM, the four wings coalesced into a blur. Optic lenses blinked as its legs left the observation platform, narrowing in on a massive blue squid-like entity that approached—the gloved hand of the lead engineer.

The hand flew toward the tiny robot, trying to capture the insect before it escaped the warehouse.

"How did it charge so quickly?" came the human voice

waveform through the insect's audio processor. *"I didn't think it would activate that fast! Place the room on lockdown, immediately!"*

Anticipating entrapment, the Firefly Mk. 1 buzzed upward, reaching an elevated height of two meters in a split second. Fueled by solar radiant light, the chrome insect paused mid-flight, switching its settings to hover-mode. The optic lenses tilted downward, zeroing in a flurry of commotion among the assembly lines. Three engineers in lab coats leaped up frantically, trying to pluck the prototype out of the air before it climbed any higher.

The nancomputer analyzed their efforts, determining the scientists were well out of range. Ignoring the turmoil, the Firefly Mk. 1 proceeded upward, its wings soaring the twenty milligram frame toward the ceiling. There, its system detected a gap in the skylight; a broken fragment in the window pane left unprepared from years earlier.

"That's a thirty million dollar investment!"

"You idiots! It's only a prototype!"

"We can't possibly know the environmental ramifications!"

It was too late.

The firefly prototype quickly departed the vicinity of the warehouse, and soon after, the state. Its movements tracked by Locke & Strider via a micro locator beacon, the robot's flight pattern was traced to its pre-programmed destination; Kansas. Its coordinates were pinpointed to a small prairie just north of Wichita, where firefly swarms were dwindling.

Once the migration was complete, Locke & Strider deployed a field expedition to monitor the insect from afar, with the goal of studying the specimen without altering the biome, according to Heisenberg's Uncertainty Principle.

It was finally spotted by the surveillance team through binoculars on the fifth night, blinking alone in an isolated field.

On the second night, two other lights were spotted.

On the third night, twenty lights were spotted.

On the fourth night, the last night the team was

scheduled to observe the specimen before the shift change, over a hundred fireflies were spotted.

In the year that followed, the official line of L&S Firefly Mk. II drones were released, now with a strategic deactivation protocol in place. Like clockwork, the swarm headed to the same field, creating an official resurgence of fireflies in Kansas. When the experiment ended and the population was sustainable without the artificial insects, a team of scientists came and collected the AI drones.

When they finally recovered the Mk. I prototype, identified by the serial number on the abdomen, the insect shell was officially put on display, transported from museum to museum. Below the glass enclosure that housed the prototype's metal exoskeleton, a plaque hung reading a simple, telling inscription, reciting the famous words of civil rights activist Ella Baker.

L&S Firefly Mk. 1
"Give light and people will find the way."

DIMENSIONAL BEND

BY

JULIAN MICHAEL CARVER

Natalya Daruk double-checked the safety on her Incinerator I9 laser pistol, peering through the ventilation grating to the dim corridor below. I9 pistols were standard issue weapons for Dimensional Bend agents. The pistols were hailed for their ability to burn through any adversary regardless of armor, while ensuring deadly accuracy.

Six rogues, just six. Three for each of us.

The corridor below was dark. Traversing through time and space often sucked significant resources from portal trams. The lights in the room were fading on and off. Emergency lighting occasionally clicked on, silhouetting both the armed guards and their captives.

To her left, Natalya could feel her rebellious protege, Regina Corviserso, staring through the grating to survey the heinous scene.

"Just six?" Regina asked arrogantly, drawing her I9. "We've handled more than that before."

"Not this tightly together," Natalya remarked, studying the bandits that patrolled the dark portal tram below. "All that back-and-forth weapons exchange could be both beneficial and deadly."

Her protege was overconfident in many high-risk situations such as this. It was a trait Natalya fervently sought to change.

Below the vent were two parallel rows of steel cages, filled with primitive half-clad men and women that grabbed at the bars. Time-travel abduction and enslavement had skyrocketed in recent years. With the emerging portal technology, shadowy corporations and wealthy terrorists sects raced to travel to the Pleistocene Epoch. There they would abduct colonies of prehistoric man, only to sell them off in the uncertain future. Dubbed 'neolithics' or 'cave dwellers' in modern times, these ancient people had rapidly become a hot commodity on the black market. It was an evil combination of slavery and sex trafficking.

With the news of another stealth portal mission spreading throughout the interim, the Dimensional Bend dispatched Natalya Daruk and Regina Corviserso to the sector where the suspected portal tram would be transmitted. Once Natalya spotted the armed guards with dark ski-masks and I60s, she confirmed the intelligence debriefing was accurate.

The transport was parked in a secluded corner of an abandoned railroad station, defunct for a hundred years. The pair of agents found a concealed corner in close proximity to the takeoff site, watching until the guards left their posts and boarded the vessel. It was only a three-car tram, with two rear cabs and a two-manned cockpit.

Natalya gritted her teeth, noting the crude spray-painted *OS* lettering on the armored siding.

The Optiverse Syndicate. I should've known.

Before the vehicle entered time-space through the generated wormhole, the two agents popped out a duct on the rear cab. The pair took turns climbing inside, seconds before it rocketed into the blue vortex.

"How many do you suspect there are in the next car?" Regina asked, keeping a careful eye on the guards below.

"Maybe two or three," Natalya guessed, "based on

what I saw before, the tram was sent through the wormhole. There may be another two in the cockpit. I don't see there being many more than that. Not for a tram of this size."

One of the taller rogues kicked at a cage, trying to intimidate a cantankerous male cave dweller. Beside the male, his mate began to weep quietly, further irritating the disgruntled mercenary.

"Will you shut that bitch up, Quentin?" asked a bearded bandit from the corner, who stood quietly against the wall smoking a fat cigar.

"I didn't know that option was on the table," answered Quentin, raising his assault weapon at the weeping female. The mercenary smiled as he clicked the safety off.

The male began to beat his chest in fury, defying his captors.

"You can't," answered another rogue from the other side of the room. "We're getting thirty-thousand a piece for each of these neolthics. If one of you hot-heads gets cute, that pay is coming out of *your* end, got it?"

"Sit your ass down and go back to your maintenance checks!" snapped Quentin, shouldering his weapon. "I'm not murdering any of them. At least not yet."

Their gruff voices echoed into the duct. The men continued arguing while conducting routine weapon checks, oblivious to the two assassins lurking above.

"Any guess as to where they're transporting them?" Regina asked, squinting through the grate.

"They're being funded by the Optiverse Syndicate," Natalya answered. "As to where the tram is headed exactly, I'm not sure. When we take it over, I can tell you it will be heading back to the Pleistocene, where these people belong."

The Optiverse Syndicate was one of many human-slave trafficking syndicates that sprung up in the past decade. Primitive slaves were in high demand, and dark web conglomerates like the Optiverse were happy to oblige—for a hefty price.

"When do you want to move?" Regina asked.

"Slide your silencer on," Natalya ordered her protege.

"The furnace will be kicking on again in a minute. It makes one hell of a racket. When it clicks on, I'll kick the vent down and we'll clear the room."

Regina nodded, threading the silencer over the chrome I9 barrel. She double-checked the magazine, confirming all nine crystal ammunition shards were allotted—a full clip.

Like clockwork, a loud humming began. The furnace roared to life, somewhere under the floors of the portal tram. Natalya raised her I9, signaling she was about to ram through the vent.

"Brace yourself," Natalya told her. "It looks like a ten-foot drop to the floor."

"Just kick the damn thing in!" Regina pressed her.

With the stamp of her boot, Natalya forced through the grate, sending both agents free-falling to the cab. As she fell, Natalya could see the baffled, disoriented faces of the humanoids from the cages.

They're probably wondering what the hell is going on!

"Hey, *whoa*, wait a *sec*—"

Quentin spun around, perplexed at the recent turn of events. The answer came from a swift I9 charge to the forehead, splitting his skull while sending him to the riveted floor.

The other rogues raced to activate their assault rifles, just as Natalya fired off rounds from her pistol. Behind her, she could hear Regina's I9 going off as well, followed by thuds of falling bodies.

The last mercenary, a man in his late twenties, raced for the alarm panel at the front of the car. He was only seconds from pushing it before Natalya's blast seared through his throat, preventing his scream. He was killed instantly.

As the firefight ceased, the endless humming of time-space travel commenced. In front of the blue streaks of the wormhole that swirled outside the windows, neolithics cheered from their cages. Some of the males shook the bars, eyes locked on the corpses of their former captors.

"We gave them quite a show," Regina remarked, helping Natalya hide the bodies from view of the next car.

"We should free them now," Natalya suggested after

they lugged Quentin's corpse away. "If we're killed, at least they'll have a fighting chance to take over the tram."

As Natalya prepared to unlock the cages, Regina grabbed her arm.

"Leave them locked for now," she said. "At least until we clear the rest of the tram. These people are millions of years old. How are we supposed to know how they'll act after they're freed?"

"Regina, we *need* to free them. We don't know what will happen to them if we're killed."

"These assholes don't know how to operate this thing?" Regina argued. "They'll probably fly it into the present and crash it into a building. Then what? More lives will be *los—*"

Before the disagreement could continue, laser blasts from an I60 rang throughout the car. Natalya pushed Regina out of the way, taking cover behind a support beam. Several mercenaries from the next car had cracked the door open, discovering that their cohorts had been dispatched. The battle for the center carriage had begun.

A few neolithics suffered wounds, howling in pain as lasers scorched their grimy flesh.

"How many?" Regina asked, ejecting a magazine from her I9 before reloading.

"Three that I can see," Natalya answered, peering around from cover. "I can see the cockpit entrance. I think the pilots locked it."

The gunmen set their weapons to burst mode, spraying a deadly flow of laser fire throughout the tram.

Natalya popped off a few rounds, tagging a gunman as he entered the room. The remaining two took cover in the next room as the automated doors shut again, temporarily halting the skirmish.

"These vents tie into the cockpit," Regina stated.

Natalya heard her ripping off a grate cover, before sliding into the opening.

"Corvisero, maybe we should wait until—"

Her protege had already vanished into the wall. For a moment, she could hear her teammate bumping through the vent before the furnace muted her footsteps.

Damn Proteges, Natalya thought.

The doors to the next car slid open again, resuming the laser conflict. Natalya chose her target carefully, putting the second man down as he swung around to deliver another blast. As he crumpled lifelessly, the final gunman tucked behind the wall. The automatic doors shut again, putting another pause on the weapons exchange.

Around her, Natalya could hear the anguish of the cave people, bantering inside their enclosures. Another two males were wounded from the last barrage.

Soon, they won't have any neolithics left to sell, Natalya thought.

She released her magazine, swapped in another, and kept her barrel trained on the sealed entrance. She anticipated another firefight to break out at any moment.

Surprisingly, the doors remained closed.

The blue vortex coalesced outside the windows as the portal tram slipped through time, journeying to a destination yet to be revealed. Behind her, Natalya could hear one of the cave children weeping, rocking back and forth on the ground.

Hang on, kid. We're not out of this yet.

Suddenly, she heard something stir in the next room. Natalya closed one eye and stared down the barrel, centering her sight on the automated door seam. When the doors parted ways, Regina was standing on the other side, relaxed and confident.

Natalya eased off the trigger, lowering the pistol.

"Wasn't too hard," remarked Corvisero, putting another round in the henchman that lay in a fetal position. The blast penetrated his skull, and the man was still.

"And the pilots?" Natalya asked, sheathing her firearm.

"Dead. No one's flying the tram and the damn driving simulator is goin' nuts. Can you operate the controls?"

"There should be a manual override."

She raced through the doors, past the middle room containing the dead Optiverse operatives and into the cockpit. The two pilots were slumped over in their chairs where Regina left them. Through the windshield, Natalya had a clear view of the blue vortex. On the dashboard, the controls were adjusted to fly forward to a programmed route. She could see the coordinates entered into a digital rectangle, with a time and location entered in a sub-menu.

"Corvisero, I don't understand?" Natalya said, studying the console. "I thought you said the controls were fried."

"I did."

She turned around, hand reaching for her pistol, only to find Regina had already raised hers. While Natalya was deciphering the controls, her protege made her move.

She hated being duped, but hated the smug look on Corvisero's face exponentially more.

"Optiverse?" Natalya asked, careful not to make any sudden movements. "Has Optiverse paid you off?"

Regina remained quiet.

"How much are they offering you?"

"They paid me enough," Regina replied, delicately petting the curved trigger.

"Now what?"

"You'll be vaporized," Regina scoffed. "Dimensional Bend will hunt me, sure, but Optiverse has already planned my disappearance. Now that these pricks are out of the way, I'll be collecting all the royalties for these neolithics."

"They'll kill you," Natalya replied. "As soon as they're done with you. They'll kill you. That's how the Optiverse does business. It's not too late to turn back, Regina. No one has to know about this."

"I know how to handle crime rings like the Optiverse," Regina smiled. "I'll be fine, trust me. Any last words?"

Natalya smiled, welcoming her death.

"You were a horrible protege," Natalya muttered, flashing a smile to her former colleague.

Regina's eyes burned.

Before she could press down on the trigger, her head lurched forward unnaturally. The weapon fell from her hands, discharging a laser blast that scorched the copilot's seat.

Regina's body slumped forward, revealing a neolithic

male standing at the cockpit entrance. In his hands, the man awkwardly held a jagged rock. Regina's blood dripped from the stone, collecting in a pool below the door frame.

Initially confused, Natalya pieced together what happened.

Sometime during one of the gunfights, a laser blast must have damaged the man's cage, allowing him to roam free once the two agents cleared the room. Before the Optiverse mercenaries abducted him, the neolithic smuggled a rock, anticipating a chance for escape.

"Thank you," Natalya muttered, unsure if the man comprehended her language. He replied with an ape-like grunt, taking a step forward. With a gentle toss, he let the bloody rock bang to the floor, landing beside Regina's body.

He reached over Natalya, grabbing a key-card from the dash before turning back to free his companions.

He's been through this morbid routine before, she assumed.

She reset the controls, steering the tram toward a different destination.

Shoving the dead captain from the chair, Natalya stared into the blue aura ahead, preparing to re-direct the tram back to the Pleistocene.

DEEP FREEZE

BY

JULIAN MICHAEL CARVER

This is what you get for shit-canning me, Treadwell!

Gritting his teeth angrily, Rick Turner stepped off his grav-car onto the rooftop of the Diamond Building, the tallest of all condominiums owned and operated by Treadwell Properties. It was a hot evening in late August, and in the Upper West Side of Manhattan, it was a record-breaking month for blistering heat. Squinting as the final rays of sunlight peaked through the skyline, Turner glanced ahead, his prize gleaming like a trophy atop the weather-beaten rooftop.

Tucked in the corner between an antenna and smokestack was the Breeze Ultimate Model Z-5 air-conditioner unit, the latest innovation in commercial real-estate cooling. Operating from a single, contained module, Z-5's were being installed all over the U.S. They had quickly become the premier AC unit for skyscrapers and apartments. Administering cool air via ten, fifteen-foot-tall canisters of liquid refrigerant hydrocarbons, the Z-5 was capable of cooling even the most complex commercial properties through several industrial-strength fans. Once the crisp air met the Z-5's massive evaporator coils, the inner turbines took over at an impressive rate of 2000 cubic feet per minute; a speed thought impossible fifty years ago. Launching air down duct work simultaneously through coordinating fans spinning at over 100 mph, the cool-down effect, known to HVAC techs as the "deep freeze", would be administered efficiently to the entire building.

It was common practice for HVAC technicians working with Z-5s to install a secondary junction box at ground level. There, residual cool air could be circulated upward, allowing the first floors of the building to feel temperature changes just as fast as occupants higher up.

Apart from their ability to bring cool air to skyscrapers almost immediately, the Breeze Ultimate Z-5s were also known for longevity. This increased lifespan was attributed to a secondary coolant of monochlorodifluoromethane, administered through automation every few hours. Lately, Turner guessed, the fluorinated hydrocarbon gas was probably applied hourly, given the intense heat the Big Apple was under. In this blistering summer, Z-5's were working overtime.

Turner had maintained, installed and operated many Breeze Ultimate units over the years for numerous corporations and condominiums. Recently, he had become so adept at troubleshooting errors with Z-5s, he often completed jobs within an hour.

Unfortunately for Treadwell Properties, through years of repairing units, he had also become adept at understanding how to make Z-5s break down.

As he worked his way up the rooftop utility stairwell to the Breeze Ultimate, he couldn't help but smile, recalling the events leading him to this point.

He first came to find gainful employment with Treadwell Properties four years earlier, after seeing a job listing for an HVAC repairmen. The company name quickly jumped out at him. CEO David Treadwell was one of the most prolific landlords in Manhattan, owning many luxurious buildings that graced the New York skyline. The company's properties were often featured in architectural magazines, gaining recognition for their sleek exteriors. Through the mid 2250's, Treadwell's empire had grown so vast, he had openly sought to develop his own in-house maintenance divisions. Eventually, the company had employed electrician teams, plumbing experts, and HVAC technicians.

Turner jumped at the listing, eager to cash in on Treadwell's empire and be a part of something reputable. Up until that point, he worked for some mid-level businesses, but not for a household name like the Fortune 100 Treadwell Properties.

As customary with large corporate interviews, the hiring process was fast and impersonal. The meeting was conducted by a young woman fresh out of college with a public-relations degree. Turner's qualifications were glanced over. Once the girl saw he was a fit, Turner was promptly offered a full-time position with outstanding benefits and a competitive wage. For four prosperous years it had been a dream job.

That all changed earlier that hot August morning.

Midway through changing refrigerant on an outdated Z-2 unit in the East Side, Turner's data tablet beeped. A web-mail icon blinked in his inbox, allegedly from CEO David Treadwell himself.

The subject bore a cryptic connotation—*To Whom It May Concern—Thanks For Four Years of Great Service.* Turner dropped his micron gauge, thumbing through the data pad as he opened the unexpected message.

The email was cold and brusque, citing immediate termination following allegations of tardiness to job sites. There was truth to this, sure. In the last year, Turner gained some seniority through several no-show employees and had occasionally taken liberties on arriving late to work. However, he was never tardy more than an hour. One such occasion—probably the one that resulted in his termination—involved his late arrival in the same building the Treadwell's were hosting the Vice President of the United States. It had been an honest delay, a matter of a failed morning alarm and fighting rush hour sky-traffic. Nonetheless, his tardiness resulted in a heated argument with Treadwell's toothy property manager, Darren Ross. The argument itself may have been forgiven, if it hadn't unfolded right in front of the Vice President's entire entourage.

Turner shook with anger as he read the straight-forward nature of the message. With a shout, he broke the data pad over his manifold device.

You wanna lay me off without as much as a week notice? Fine! But not after you pay!

It took only an hour to formulate his revenge.

He would park his grav-car on the roof of the prestigious Treadwell-owned Diamond Building, the company's crowning achievement in Manhattan. Once there, he would dismantle the Z-5's cooling protocol. Without the unit pumping cool air, the building's occupancy would swelter in the August heat wave. Treadwell would be bombarded with angry phone calls. When they would finally send a repairmen to fix the unit, they would find the components sabotaged beyond understanding. This would require a new unit ordered. Shipping the new unit would take a minimum of two weeks due to supply shortages. Two weeks in the hottest month of the year, and in one of the *hottest* years in recorded history.

For shits and giggles, Turner would also lock the rooftop door from the outside, making inspecting the unit impossible without flying a grav-car up. That part wasn't glamorous, he knew, but every inconvenience he could pass onto Treadwell, the better.

"Probably fired me for younger blood with cheaper salaries," Turner grumbled, preparing his tool bag for tampering with the Z-5's control pad. "Well, Mr. Treadwell, the least I can do is get you some angry web-mail from tenants. Hey, if this all goes well, maybe they'll even torch you in the 'Times. *Ah,* that would just be the cherry on top!"

He grabbed the tools needed for sabotage before climbing the ladder of the twenty-foot-tall Z-5. There, he used a drill to unscrew the mesh grating, exposing condenser coils, coolant fluid lines and large fans tucked in the shaft.

Excellent.

He turned to the sky. No grav-cars were flying in the upper lanes. In a panic, he scanned the rooftop of the Diamond Building. Thankfully, Treadwell hadn't installed any cameras, prohibiting security from witnessing his sophomoric crime.

All set, he smiled. *Treadwell will have his suspicions, but he'll never be able to pin anything on me! Should've put cameras up, ol' man.*

He worked swiftly, clogging the coolant lines, dismantling evaporator coils, and removing expansion valves. Then he moved to the electrical components, snipping exposed wiring and cables tucked in junction boxes.

Finally, the gentle whine of the fan began to wane. The Z-5 was officially shutting down. Within the hour, he speculated, the building would become unbearably hot.

It might not even take that long, given the blistering heat from the streets and high humidity. Job well done, Turner.

He leaned forward, retrieving a vise grip clamped to a coolant line. When doing so, he felt a weight leave his shirt pocket. To his horror, he saw a chrome blur whisk past his head—his grav-car key fob. The fob plummeted down toward the deep well of the Z-5. Turner knew if the fob fell below the first turbine, it would be unrecoverable.

Anxiety high, his instincts kicked in. Thrusting his hand down, he tried to wretch the keys from falling, missing the fob by mere inches.

HISSSSS!

"*Auugghhh!*"

With a blue puff of pressurized monochlorodifluoromethane vapor, the Z-5's deep freeze port flared over his hand. Frostbite consumed his right hand to his elbow. The frigid substance applied pain and numbness to the limb as the hydrocarbons performed their terrible task.

"*Nooo!* Damn! Damn you!"

In his rush to sabotage his former employer, Turner forgot the first rule of HVAC in the twenty-third century; a rule so important it was the first thing they taught in trade school—deactivate the Freon spray ports.

First manufactured in the 2100's, Freon ports exhibited an extra puff of refrigerant spray for an expedited cooling effect via vapor valves. Unfortunately, these valves resulted in several incidents with technicians who forgot to deactivate the ports. The accidents were particularly problematic during winter repairs, when the climate was already dangerously cold.

Turner tumbled backwards, watching as his hand became encased in ice crystals. He thrust the static limb into the sunlight, hoping the temperature would quickly thaw the frost. Underneath, the appendage went limp. He struggled to stand. Moving the arm felt like swaying a thousand-pound dumbbell.

"No! *Nooo!*"

He rushed off the Z-5, awkwardly hobbling down the ladder with his one functioning hand. The clever plan of sabotage had gone to hell. All that mattered was escaping before a passerby witnessed his crime.

In a clumsy dash, he hobbled to his grav-car. With the fob lost, his only hope of entering the vehicle was the fingerprint scanner on the driver-side door. Slamming his left thumb against the scanner, Turner saw a digital green line descend over his thumbprint. Inside the nano-computer, algorithms conducted security processes to decide if unlocking the door was calculable.

Turner withdrew his thumb. A loading symbol popped up, spinning in a seamless loop while the computer processed user-input. To his shock, a single blip rang out from the speakers, followed by two simple words on the ID scanner—access denied.

"*No!* This can't be *happen—*"

Then he remembered something; a critical flaw that bit him in the ass. Months earlier, when he bought the grav-car in Brooklyn, he recalled the overweight pushy salesman trying to describe the importance of setting up two-thumb access authentication. It was a backup function installed in the event one thumb was injured. In haste, he failed to set up two-thumb authentication. To make matters worse, he also forgot to set up the retina scan, the index finger scan, or a PIN number. The grav-car, his only inconspicuous way off the rooftop, had become inaccessible.

Even if he could depart the roof through the doorway, his grav-car would still be parked there. Once the sky-police ran the plates, it wouldn't take Treadwell long to discover his plan, given the effects of the broken Z-5 would soon transpire.

When tenants started lamenting the heat in the Diamond Building, Treadwell wouldn't wait to send a repairmen up. Turner's dastardly plan would be exposed for the world to see.

Fine! Just get me off the roof! Maybe I can have a grav-tow get my ship down before the building overheats. Where's the exit!? There!

On the corner of the roof, an orange bulb shined over a utility door to the building's inner stairwell.

Eighty-some floors all the way down. Don't take the elevator; there will be cameras! Okay, just get the descent over with, Turner!

Scooping up his belongings, Turner made a dash for the alcove. Above, the Z-5 began to spark. His tampering was beginning to take hold.

Just get to the lower levels! Get a grav-tow up here, then I'll be scott-free! Hopefully until then, no one sees my ship, and—

His hand enclosed on the door handle. He gave it a hearty tug, a chill creeping up his spine as the door groaned against hinges. It wouldn't budge.

"You've gotta be shittin' me!"

Turner's heart sank. He slid away from the alcove, letting the tool bag tumble to the roof slate floor. Locked. Locked from the inside. He was trapped; marooned on a skyscraper rooftop with the crime and getaway vehicle all bundled together. He felt like a rodent caught in a mouse-trap, inches from the glob of delicious peanut butter, only to die before tasting its creamy delight.

Toast. Ruined. Jailed for vandalism, trespassing, property damage. Maybe even arson if the unit catches fire.

Above, the Z-5 let fly a flurry of sparks. Billowy smoke climbed from the shaft, probably originating from where he snipped circuitry. Soon, fire grav-ships would see the smoke and ascend, notifying Treadwell of the incident.

Hands flew into his graying hair, massaging his forehead to quell the oncoming headache. An anxiety attack beckoned, hinted by his rapid breaths and pounding heart. His arm ached, encased in a glaze of frostbite.

The pain, both physical and mental, was excruciating.

What if a fire starts? What if it spreads through the vents? What if someone gets hurt? No one was meant to get hurt! It was just meant to be a nuisance to Treadwell! Just a last revenge for getting laid off! Ugh, this frostbite is killing me! Why did I go through with it? Why? Wh–

Suddenly his pocket buzzed.

It was his Treadwell Properties-issued data phone. He forgot he was still in possession of the device. It should've been given to corporate earlier when he delivered his uniform and company-issued gear.

The caller ID came up. It was none other than business mogul David Treadwell himself, his former employer.

Oh, God! How can he know already? Does he have a freakin' crystal ball I don't know about?!

Cautiously he pressed *Answer.* He lifted the glowing device up to his ear, bracing for the worst.

"Hello?" he cringed, eyes shut as if he'd be punched through the LCD screen.

"Turner? Hi, it's Dave Treadwell. Hope I didn't catch you at a bad time. I know it's after hours, but this can't wait. It was a mistake letting you go. Some screw-up in middle-management or HR. Those assholes sign my name on anything, even without my authorization. Anyway, you were *never* meant to get laid off, just put on brief sabbatical. Listen, I've had a few people quit on me in HVAC in the past weeks. It's been hell finding replacements. I need you back, and I'll double your pay with a promotion to manager for the entire HVAC division. You're a damn fine technician, Turner. You know your shit, and I can't afford to lose you. How's all that sound?"

"*Ahhh*", Turner gasped, unsure what was happening. "Sounds good, Sir?"

"Just call me David. Dave, even. Listen, work never sleeps. People in the Diamond Building have been complaining about lapses in cooling for the past week. Lights have been dimming, the start-up-assist has been shoddy; the whole nine yards. I thought the yuppie bozos fixed it last week, but this evening it must've went royally haywire. The whole building is losing cool-air. Some people on the upper floors even experienced power failure. Now thermostats aren't accurately displaying temperature changes. Of course, this would happen in the *hottest* month of the year. Are you free to make a late night house call to deal with this? I'm assuming you at least have some gear of your own."

"I'm already en route, sir," Turner smiled, completely bewildered by the twist of fate.

"Excellent. Call me when it's resolved so I can announce it to the tenants. I have a lot of angry people that need an apology. Got a few calls that sounded like they were coming with torches and pitch-forks!"

"I'll have it fixed up in a jiffy sir," Turner said, mentally preparing himself for repairing a sabotaged Z-5 with one arm and a splitting headache. "Oh, and sir?"

"Yes, Turner?"

"Please keep your phone on you. I'll be able to make it to the Diamond Building and get to the unit for repair, but my grav-ship has been faulty. I've been meaning to get a new power converter and battery, but haven't gotten to the dealership yet. I might need picked up by grav-taxi. Quite possibly, I might also need a grav-tow. If I'm in a pinch, can I call you?"

"Of course, Turner. Anything you need. You've totally saved my ass. Keep up the good work and let me know if you need anything. Not that I can offer much now that most HVAC techs quit. But yes, I have my phone. Let me know if you get stuck up there. I'll send help."

"Yes, sir. Have a good night."

"You too, Turner. Thanks."

The call ended. Turner frowned, staring at the damage he wrought.

The control panel for the Z-5 had gone dark; that alone might take ten minutes to resolve. The vandalized components inside would take even longer. Thankfully, Turner knew exactly where to patch the problems to cool the building.

Nothing a roll of electrical tape won't fix!

He hustled back up the ladder with an awkward hobble, with only one question in mind.

Can I repair this damn unit before my arm needs amputated.

He arrived at the Z-5 tower grate, going hard at work to salvage the unit. Making due with one arm, Turner took his time, making a mental note to deactivate the Freon spray.

BINARY LIBRARY

BY

JULIAN MICHAEL CARVER

"I'm sorry, but the data tablet is *long* overdue."

"I'm telling you, it's not. I returned it last year."

"The system is displaying zero inventory on that item. I assure you, our server doesn't lie. If you've misplaced it, you can buy the library another copy and I can remove the hold on your account."

Artieus grunted angrily. He was about to lose his temper; he hated that about himself. Getting angry over such a trivial thing like a stop-hold on withdrawing from the virtual library.

It was a mistake on the library's part; he was sure of it. He remembered returning the data tablet in question—*101 Techniques for Ionic Electrostatic Glider Propulsion*—last year. He remembered it vividly because the trip wasted half his lunch break at the glider repair shop, causing him to return with a bitter attitude.

"Until you return the data tablet, you can't check out any more tablets at this library," the librarian, an older woman named Vivian, said sternly. "I'm sorry. Rules are rules."

Artieus could feel his fists turning into knuckles. He wasn't angry for having to buy the library a new data tablet. Data tablets were quite cheap, only several credits. His anger stemmed from someone telling him he made a mistake.

"It's a data tablet," he continued, trying to keep a calm composure. "It's basically a holographic digital hardcover with a built-in processor. When pages are flipped, micro-alternators charge the batteries. You're telling me there's no tracking device on these pieces of junk?"

"I'm afraid not," Vivian replied. "Normally, people don't cause quite a stir when they're asked to buy a new one."

"I can prove that it's here," he said, "If you'll take me to where it's shelved, I guarantee you'll find the tablet is safely logged in the system."

"I can assure you, it *isn't*," Vivian went on, leering at him behind wide-rimmed spectacles. "If it was, it'd be plugged into the network circuit and there would be a record of it in the database. But just to satisfy your curiosity, I'll take you to it. If it was here, the system indicates it would be on floor 12, shelf 27b."

"Thank you," Artieus said as Vivian walked toward the lift.

The elevator ride up was astounding. Staring out the all-glass facade of the newly installed elevator, Artieus took in the breadth of the building. The library had been built in an old university cathedral; the newer books were converted into modern data tablets and were housed on the lower levels. The older tablets that faded from prominence were shipped higher up. The elevator passed the eighth floor, where the lift eased into an enclosed shaft, cutting off the wider view of the lower cathedral. Finally, the doors opened to floor twelve.

Artieus stepped out, shocked at the sight.

Comprised of seemingly endless aisles of dusty shelves, the twelfth floor was desolate. Most of the data racks were blinking with dying battery life. A few of the data tablets were dimming, indicating that, without their page alternators being flipped, their charging cells would soon need replaced. Unlike the bustling lower levels, the only noise of the twelfth floor came from the whine of overworked computer fans.

"Does anyone come up here?" Artieus asked, following Vivian off the lift.

"We get up here when we can," Vivian informed him. "These backlogged data tablets aren't checked out as often."

A minute later they arrived at the twenty-seventh aisle. Like the other aisles, most of the data tablets shelved into their ports were dimming with low-battery life. A few were missing altogether, and more were stacked unattended in crates that needed offloaded.

"As you can see," Vivian began, scanning the aisle, "Your data tablet is still miss—"

"Found it!" Artieus announced, pointing to a shelf with a bright smile.

A data tablet with a spine that read *101 Techniques for Ionic Electrostatic Glider Propulsion* was sticking out of its port, lodged at an awkward angle. He could see from the spine that the battery cells were running low. Artieus guessed that since the day he returned it, it was hastily inserted back into its port on the twelfth floor, albeit incorrectly, allowing the power on the tablet to drain over time. Since it hadn't been reinserted into the port, Artieus guessed that was the reason the network wasn't displaying a record of it.

"Oh my," Vivian frowned, shoving the tablet into its port correctly. "I'm *so* sorry! I rarely make a mistake like this. I'm guessing one of the newer clerks did this. The younger help isn't what it used to be. You see, no one reads anymore. I think kids nowadays just don't have the patience or concentration for it. Because of this, I don't think the younger clerks care as much. No wonder it didn't register in the database."

Artieus felt the anger wash out of him, relieved he had been correct.

"Reading has become a thing of the past," he smiled. "I think you're right. The youth of today just can't concentrate on reading, especially with all the VR games and galactic travel. They lead busy lives. So, since I'm one of these rare *readers* as we call them, and since my data tablet *is* where I thought it'd be, am I allowed to resume checking out tablets?"

"Of course you can," Vivian smiled. "Let's get back downstairs. The twelfth floor gives me the creeps."

"I thought it was just me," he smiled, following her back to the lift.

CHILDREN OF THE MONOLITH

BY

JULIAN MICHAEL CARVER

"*Here they come!*" I heard Stephen cry, amid the shrieks of the vile, wretched humanoids.

Running in utter terror, I fell flat on my face, turning in time to see my partner, Stephen Rames, mobbed up by the green beings. The monsters blended perfectly into the dense jungle, covered in dried leaves and caked with mud. From all angles they emerged from the thicket, wrapping him from all sides. Instantly his space-suit was defiled, slathered in muck as the creatures tackled him, cackling with howls of delight at their next savory meal.

"*Stephen!*" I managed to scream.

Grief-stricken and fearing for my life, I waddled away, watching as the humanoids weighed him down.

"Take the samples!" he cried suddenly, stripping himself of his backpack and thrusting the luggage toward me. I caught it and regained my footing, backing away further as my mind spiraled into a state of shock. Many of the creatures swarmed in through the sides, securing Stephen from escaping while encircling from the front.

Others swung down from above, using vines as a crude means of transportation. Several humanoids turned to face me, leering with gnarled fangs and yellow eyes, deciding if I was worth the effort.

Within seconds, they did.

"I'm sorry!" I shouted as tears began to fall. Sobbing and staving off a panic-attack, I threw my backpack over my shoulder and bounded into the jungle. Fighting hysteria, I tried to ignore the fact that I left my partner behind to die—to be devoured by the strange race of jungle carnivores.

I could hear them following me, bounding along on all fours as if their evolution prohibited bipedal motion. In the distance, I heard Stephen's bloodcurdling screams as he was devoured by the wicked race. I tried not to picture it, but his cries were so loud, it was nearly impossible. I imagined his body left to rot under the hot jungle sun, stranded on a foreign planet without a proper burial.

Coming to PX-178 was a mistake! Why did we risk it? We needed more support! It was a mistake! All a big mistake!

The mission was a failure from the start; two probes had been lost as our shuttle touched down, dooming us without drone aerials of our surroundings; an act that prevented accurate assessments of the topography. A bad case of food poisoning on the orbiting station left only Stephen and I to touch down on the planet. Within an hour we got what we came here for: water samples to measure salinity and TDS levels, soil samples needed for pH level testing, and rock core samples to gauge the planet's geological age.

On the way back to our ship, that's where it all went awry. Stephen, whose paranoia was renowned and lampooned on the station, was the first to notice we were being tailed. At first, I really didn't think much of it. Sure, we were strangers on a strange land—no pun intended. Fauna were bound to be curious. I tried to calm him down, and it worked for a little, until we saw what was *actually* tailing us: a group of maybe twenty or thirty five-meter tall human-like creatures. They were nude, save for where the jungle foliage slathered over their bony bodies with mud.

Stephen was the first to observe they were unmistakably canine, mouths full of sharp incisors. Their culture was primitive; so primitive that they hadn't figured out how to sharpen sticks into spears. *Probably pack hunters*, I guessed, relying on sheer numbers to trap their prey, rather than ingenuity through weaponry.

Unfortunately, we soon discovered our analysis was correct.

The creatures sprang at us, mouths agape with serrated teeth.

By sheer luck, we broke free of their initial trap. In our reckless flight to the shuttle, I heard them howling in despair. Before long, I realized it was less of a lamenting wail and more of a hunting signal. More of the strange race heard the call, joining in like a pack of hungry hyenas. As we ran, I could hear the savages jostling through the jungle, sprinting furiously to cut off our escape. They caught up to us a mile from the gorge where we parked our shuttle. That's when they attacked—where they took Stephen.

Now it's just me. Okay, Jazelle! Don't think, just run. You get the strato-jumper back to the station, then you can radio the Union for help. Maybe Stephen can still be saved...

At that instant, I heard a large bumbling neanderthal hot on my heels, grunting like a madman. The cretin came within inches of latching onto my backpack.

Where did these accursed monsters come from!? Are they some horrible accident of evolution gone wrong? Or just a millennia of inbreeding within a dying culture.

The backstory of the strange race of carnivores didn't matter. All that mattered was escape. Escape to orbit. Escape to where I could regroup and mount a rescue mission for Stephen—if he was still even alive.

With a loud howl behind me, I diverted my sprint to the right. The first humanoid tried to snag my backpack with a dive, failing miserably before crashing into a bush. Two of the males broke off, following my reckless descent down a grade littered with vines and scraggly bushes. Frantically I weaved through vegetation, trying to confuse the humanoids and throw more obstacles in their path. Undaunted, they crashed through the thicket, hellbent on cutting off my escape even if it meant gravely injuring themselves in the process.

A silver glimmer through the canopy gave me hope—the chrome hull of the strato-jumper. The ground leveled as I broke for the ship, barely visible through the foliage thirty steps ahead.

In the chaos I looked back. Two carnivores were hot on my heels, with a third limping to catch up.

"*Damn you!*" I cried, knowing the humanoids don't comprehend my alien dialect.

They responded in violent grunts between laborious breaths, exhausted from the chase but determined in their resolve.

I tore through the last traces of the thicket, emerging into the clearing. The strato-jumper loomed ahead, glistening in red afternoon rays like a trophy. Behind, the foliage erupted. I heard the humanoids burst onto the gorge, emitting barbaric cackles while galloping to envelop me.

When I felt their hot rancid breath raking my neck, I knew they had me.

"*Oooph!*" I cried as the first neanderthal sacked me from behind.

The creature's hairy arms wrapped around my waist. I fell forward into the rocky gorge, only five feet from the strato-jumper's extended ramp.

Stars exploded. The last thing I felt were the callous hands of the humanoids pulling me back toward the jungle. As my consciousness waned, I caught one last look at the shuttle before it became obscured by palm fronds, before slipping away to whatever festering hole the cretins dragged me to.

Huh?

The docile blades of a wooden ceiling fan were the first thing I saw, spinning before a white ceiling. Reddish sunlight of the golden hour descended over my face, forcing me to squint. There was a sweet smell of ocean mist on the air, and a cadence created from the distant cawing of seagulls. It was, quite possibly, the most 'at peace' I've ever felt.

Is this my version of an afterlife?

I lurched to an upright position, realizing I am sitting in a bed of clean linen. The room wasn't particularly large, maybe twenty by twenty feet, comprised of white walls bearing several paintings and sculptures. A singe open window faced the setting sun, where the waves of the ocean washed up onto a idyllic cove some hundred meters below. I sluggishly stood out of bed and peered out, ascertaining an impossible climb to the base. The building was a metallic tower, built of reflective panels and random utility ports where circuitry could be accessed.

It's the same sun! I'm still on PX-178—that savage planet! But where am I? Am I rescued?

I winced, feeling my head. The wound I attained when the humanoids tackled me had been bandaged heavily with gauze. Some scratches on my arms were also bandaged, and my dirty space-suit had been exchanged for a clean white gown.

I even smell good! Have I been washed?

To the right, an open door emptied to a hallway. There were no sounds, save for the gentle hum of automated fans within the vents. The building came from a culture far more advanced than the humanoids, yet bore an outdated feel to the technology I was accustomed to. The vague abstract artwork on the walls gave little clues to the building's origins.

My curiosity had run wild.

What the hell is this place?

In a dream-like euphoria, I wandered out from the recovery suite, faced by a sterile white hallway. The passage took several sharp turns. A minute into my journey, an open doorway appeared to the right. I cautiously peered in, cursing that my presence was immediately seen.

"Well, you're *finally* awake! Come in! Please, come

in."

The sight was so visually different from the humanoids, it almost startled me. I quickly relaxed, realizing this was my rescuer.

Sitting at the far end of a large oval glass table was a man. Trimmed in angelic white and bronze robes and short-cropped gray hair, he looked almost divine. In front of him throughout the oval table was a majestic banquet of food; rolls, steaks, hams, salad, potatoes, and deserts—all kinds of deserts which I hadn't tasted since our operation left Earth.

I salivated just looking at the royal feast, and for a second, I wondered if I had been flown back to the United States.

"Please, sit," the man gestured to a chair on my side of the table. I complied, albeit cautiously, wondering why this man had rescued me and why I was being fed the banquet of a queen.

"Thanks," I said, shoving a large roll into my mouth.

The taste was heavenly, exquisite, and seemed to melt in my mouth.

"*I*... I don't know what to say."

"You're hungry," the man said with a warm smile. "You've been out cold for three days. My nurse is gonna flip that you finally woke up. She's been hoping to talk to you. We all have."

"*We?*" I asked, suddenly fearful. "You don't mean those monsters in the jungle?"

"Oh, the Marwaks?" he chuckled, brushing aside my fears. "No, not them. I'm talking about *my* people. There's too few of us left now I'm afraid. Most of us are past sixty, and none of our offspring are bearing children. We are a dying culture on an empty planet, but we take pride in what we've built. I'm sorry, allow me to introduce myself. My name is Prima. I'm the council-appointed prefect of Apollo, our self-contained city named after the Grecian sun god. The name stuck after what we've constructed."

"And Apollo is where I'm at now?" I asked, cautiously chewing a delicious slice of smoked ham.

"Correct," Prima smiled. "You are in Apollo, actually pretty near the top of the complex. The only six floors above us are some apartments, my quarters, and the watchtower rooftop. That's where my scout saw your shuttle land. We've been waiting for you—or anyone—rather, for a long time."

"Who are you people?" I asked, shoving in an entire spoonful of mashed potatoes.

"I suppose we've never taken on a formal name," Prima answered thoughtfully. "We broke away from the Union a century ago, questing for a life of simplicity and contentment. Our ancestors departed from the Union via several drop ships and landed here on PX-178. We're told from our history passed down to us, they grew tired of the warmongering and infighting that ran rampant in Union worlds. We are a peace-loving people, appreciative of the arts and culture. We've lived here ever since, in a self-sustaining solar-powered monolith constructed by my grandfather, salvaged from pieces of their arrival fleet."

"This is quite a large feast," I said, sipping fine wine. "Is it all for you?"

"No," Prima chucked, drinking from his own chalice. "More will come. I just had a hunch you'd be waking up soon. I didn't want the others to join until you had a chance to adjust. I'm sorry your arrival was rather—*uh*, less than pleasant. But we're happy the marwaks got you here safe and sound, minus a few bruises."

I dropped the chalice, shattering the glass on the floor as I stood from my chair. My heart was beating non-stop as I pieced together the horrible truth: Prima and the Apollo culture were in league with the savage humanoids that dragged me here. The same humanoids that killed Stephen.

"Calm down, please," Prima stood, gesturing back to the seat with his hands. "They aren't dangerous. They dropped you off at the entrance, where our guards carried you inside. You see; the marwaks are the original heirs of this world. When our people landed and built the monolith, we negotiated a treaty. We engage in commerce with the marwaks, providing them with vegetables and crops from the outer gardens in exchange for livestock and fish they bring. I know they look like man-eaters, but they surprisingly *love* vegetables. Some of them can even speak very broken English; our translators have been working with their alphas to improve communication. I know they can come off rather brash and dominant, but they're harmless. They knew we were looking for you, so they brought you to our doors. Wasn't that kind of them?"

I took a step backward, but not before considering reaching for the steak knife for protection. Prima took a step toward me, a look of worry washing away the formerly pleasant smile.

"Please don't run!" he pleaded, trying to circumnavigate the large table. "Really, it's all a misunderstanding!"

I turned to flee—running squarely into the chest of a man.

"There you are!" a familiar voice said. "We were all wondering when you were going to wake up."

I looked up at the man's face, back-lit by the rays of reddish sunlight flooding through the hallway.

Immediately, my thoughts retracted to my prior theory; I had entered the afterlife.

"*Stephen!*" I shrieked, clutching his robed shoulders in disbelief. "You're... you're *alive?*"

"Of course!" he exclaimed with a big smile, "Plus or minus some bruises. I guess we're lucky the marwaks are friendly to humans. Although, I wish they didn't weigh as much; kinda hurt when they dog-piled me. I was happy to find out they're just big teddy bears."

"Okay, tell me now," I said, turning sideways to face both my friend and Prima. "What the hell is going on? Why were we brought here?"

"It might be easier to show you," Prima smiled, gesturing to a side door in the dining hall. "Follow me, and I'll show you why we were so anxious to bring you here."

He started to walk away. I turned to Stephen, who nodded that it was safe to follow. Cautiously, I followed the prefect through the archway. Behind, Stephen's reassuring hand rested calmly on my shoulder.

A second later, the three of us were standing on a balcony with a breathtaking view. The landscape was so beautiful, I instantly forgot about the marwaks.

As I took a place beside Prima, my jaw fell open at the sheer beauty of the sight.

To the left, the seas washed peaceful waves over a golden cove; the same view from the recovery suite. The beach ran a hundred meters until it transitioned into a treeline. The treeline became a small forest which grew to the base of the Apollo monolith, where small walls and lower-level metallic buildings were erected. The buildings were ornate, carved with precision from stone, inset with chromatic solar-capturing features to harness the sunlight. I could see farmland there, where minuscule humans tilled the earth. Others were providing utility support, working at electrical junction stations and troubleshooting network cables. From the mountain to my right, a large aqueduct flowed from near the summit, spilling water into a large man-made lagoon on the other side of the monolith, churned by a mill wheel outside a treatment facility.

"It's incredible," I said in awe, mesmerized by the culture. "You've accomplished so much with so few. I feel so at peace here. It's astounding what you've built here, Prima."

"And that brings me to you," he went on, turning toward them, "And why we've brought you here. I've already briefed Stephen, so now I'll fill you in. Have a look up, will you?"

I did. To my surprise, right over my head was a massive stone sculpture of a young woman's head, mounted to the side of the monolith that faced the setting sun. With time, the face had withered, leaving the sculpture with unflattering indentations. Nonetheless, her youthful beauty was evident, aglow with waning traces of red sunlight.

"Oh my God," I gawked, jaw dropping at the stunning masterpiece. "She's *astounding*. A true work of art; whoever carved it."

"It's my grandmother," Prima smiled, beaming with pride. "In her younger years, as a stone mason remembered her. Her and my grandfather colonized this world. When the monolith was constructed, the colonists decided both her face and my grandfather's would grace the pinnacle. It took some time to build, from what I was told. Can you imagine getting that stone all the way to the top of the tower? I still don't know how they did it. It's a mystery, even to this day."

"And you want *me* to fix it?" I asked. "You must be mistaken. I'm a geological scientist, not a stone mason."

"We don't want you to fix it," Prima grinned. "We want you to be the new face. We'll be chiseling it down in the coming months, and are looking for another model to be the new face of the Apollo monolith. You see, we're all getting older. Our artists need a youthful face for the project. Stephen has already volunteered to become the new face for my grandfather, and has already given us the required cast. Now, we just need you, Jazelle."

"I take it Stephen told you my name," I laughed, elbowing my friend. "You couldn't have just asked us *politely* to model for you? You had to send an entire horde of jungle freaks after us?"

Prima gave a pleasant smile.

"As I said," he went on. "We're all elders here now. There would've been no way to have caught up with you. We had no choice but to rely on our alliance with the marwaks."

I smiled back, taking one last glance at the withering visage mounted to the Apollo monolith.

"I'd be delighted to give you my cast," I said finally. "Just promise me that after I do, your people will safely escort us back to the shuttle. I'd like to get there in one piece this time."

"Beautiful and funny," Prima chuckled, gesturing to the banquet hall. "You have my word; a safe return in exchange for a lifetime of immortality in the form of our sculpture. Now come! Let's finish the feast and get you to the molding room. Our stone masons are *very* eager to commence the project."

WATCH YOUR SIX!

BY

JULIAN MICHAEL CARVER

"Behind you!" Sergeant Kieran Riggs screamed through the tactical comm channel, watching in terror as the glowing green ray launched overhead.

Before his colleagues in the forward position could respond, the green blast from the Pulverizer eradicated the hover-track fifty meters ahead. The vehicle, carrying as many as eight soldiers and his CO—Colonel Adam Mitro—exploded into shrapnel. The blast converted the plate-steel exterior to metal shards and the occupants to festering goo.

Kieran raced to swerve his hover-track, arcing the vehicle to the right while bellowing warnings to his accompanying vehicle; a hover-tank with a dual barreled chemical-laser turret. Both vehicles floored it across the war-torn salt flats toward the open holo-gate. There, the last traces of humanity awaited behind the sanctuary of an underground bunker, plotting their last stand against the invading Dul'ruak. Once through the holo-gate, both transports would find refuge from the bombardment of the Pulverizer, the latest innovation of human-killing technology. The base was reinforced with tungsten-coated plate rivets—a metal that proved adept at deflecting Dul'ruak bombardments.

"Come on, you hunk of *scrap!*" Kieran thought, slamming a gloved fist on the hover-track's dash. "Don't give out on me now!"

"Juan, how far is it?" he shouted to his gunner, just ten feet behind on a motorized swivel turret.

"Three *clicks!*" Corporal Juan Rodriguez replied, ramming open the firing safety for his plasma launching eight-barrel mini-gun. "Maybe even two! Shit, Lieutenant, that is one big mother *fu*—"

"Just start firing!" Kieran shouted back, blinking grains of sand from his eyes as he ripped toward the holo-gate. "Weapons free! Open fire! *Open fire!*"

"On it!" Juan snapped, peering down the sight.

The sounds of the plasma being ionized and converted to knife-sized projectiles erupted over the groaning hover-track engine. Through the side mirrors, Kieran watched as Juan's blue tracers zipped skyward, sailing toward the warship code-named Pulverizer.

The Dul'ruak battle-cruiser was a web of interlocking obsidian cubes, culminating in a pyramidal cockpit toward the bow. The warship boasted an impressive armament, including fifty laser turrets and automated short-range missile silos. Its primary weapon was a large under-mounted death ray; a nuclear-pumped 200 kW laser weapon of unfathomable power.

A hundred humans perished while attaining the blueprints for the weapon, killed while evacuating the nearby Dul'ruak development plant. Now, only two vehicles of the human mission remained, each with duplicate data-discs presumably containing the blueprints for the ultimate weapon now being fitted to Pulverizer ships. It was an ironic race against time. Both human-piloted vehicles were carrying the only secret to beat their enemy's innovation, while being targeted by that weapon's exact prototype.

It's only a matter of time, Kieran swallowed, fearing

another blast from the death ray.

To his terror, Juan's rounds whisked off an invisible deflector shield enveloping the warship, scattering the plasma shards in all directions. The Pulverizer, undaunted by the blasts, proceeded across the flats. To his right, the hover-tank let fly three quick blasts from its dual-barrel plasma raygun. Sailing from the turret, the blasts exploded over the warship's ghostly bubble. The blasts were then absorbed into the force field through glowing ripples, until the color drained from the plasma charge.

Kieran could hardly believe his eyes. The force field was essentially taking enemy firepower and converting it to a local power source.

"The Dul'ruaks are getting creative!" Juan shouted as his mini-gun overheated. "Invisible deflector shields that absorb our firepower into direct energy."

"You gotta be shittin' me!" Kieran gasped, staring in the mirror.

On the bottom of the warship, the Pulverizer's primary weapon—the 20 kW death ray—was gearing up for another charge. A turbulent green ball of coherent energy had generated in the massive twenty-meter-long barrel. In the cockpit, he noticed several silhouettes of Dul'ruak warriors and strategists pointing at the pair of fleeing vehicles, deciding which would be worthy of annihilation. A second later, Kieran watched as the laser cannon pivoted right, painting the hover-tank as the target.

"Black Knight One, you're being *target*—"

With a sound of a blaring locomotive, the Pulverizer launched a second blast from the death ray. The smoldering sky glowed green as the laser photons deployed, searing into the fleeing hover-tank. Instantly the vehicle ignited in a rambunctious fireball, depleted to a frenzy of flaming gears and rivets that skittered in all directions.

"*Augh!*" Juan cried, toppling onto the floor of the hover-track.

"*Ugh!*" Kieran grunted.

Shards from the tank's explosion bombarded his side door, forcing him to veer the vehicle off course. Fighting to regain his trajectory, he spun the wheel back to a straight line, ramming his foot down on the accelerator pedal as they careened toward the holo-gate. Behind, the Pulverizer continued its imminent approach, passing the first hover-track's fiery scrap pile.

"I hope those sons a' bitches keep that holo-gate open!" Juan cried, regaining his stance as he turned back to the plasma mini-gun.

"You spoke too soon!" Kieran shouted, spying motion ahead.

As if on queue, both edges of the massive fifty-meter-tall gate began to close with a hazy glow. An ionized field of translucent air-plasma comprised of blue light photons began to slide across both edges of the gate. The barriers proceeded toward the middle where they would eventually meet, sealing the entrance behind holographic stabilization.

"They're lockin' us out?" Juan shrieked, fixing the bolt tracks on his mini-gun.

"No," Kieran yelled back, flooring the accelerator, "They know we can either make it at our present speed, or we'll burn up from the Dul'ruak's next blast. They're giving us just enough time to punch through before they seal off the Pulverizer!"

"The Dul'ruak's are chargin' it up!" Juan screamed, voice faltering in fright before letting fly another barrage of futile plasma shards.

Kieran glanced in the mirror, confirming Juan's cryptic observation. The death ray was initializing another green orb, welling to the size of a small house. The glowing sphere was as beautiful as it was deadly; a ball of self-conduced lightning stemming from a central pulsating aura.

It would be only seconds before the Dul'ruak's weapon would be unleashed on them.

"It's gonna be close! We're running out of time! Come on, you bastard. *Faster!*"

He turned back to the flats. The holo-gate flew at them, but would it be fast enough?

Kieran rammed the accelerator, cringing as the actuators moaned under the hover-track's rickety frame.

"They're opening fire!" Juan cried out, leaping off the swivel turret to the bed of the track.

In a flash, the Pulverizer's laser cannon went off again, brightening the sky like a green thunderstorm—just as Kieran swerved the hover-track through the holo-gate's narrow barrier.

"Yes! *AHA!*" Juan screeched like a lunatic, fist pumping the air.

In the rear-view, he observed the Dul'ruak's blast whisk toward them, only to be intercepted by the holo-gate's sealed air plasma.

Glad to be alive, Kieran slammed on the brakes and swerved the vehicle around, facing the holo-gate. Dozens of soldiers, guards, and personnel swarmed their vehicle and watched the entrance. The Pulverizer approached, paused, and waited—before starting a clockwise turn. As the warship turned back to the Dul'ruak side of the DMZ, a flurry of applause rang out.

Kieran and Juan were yanked out from the hover-track like a pair of rock stars at a concert.

"Congratulations, gentlemen," General Stafford announced as the crowd parted, allowing him up to the vehicle's hood. "You encountered the enemy's secret weapon and lived to fight another day."

"Forgive me, Sir," Kieran saluted, exiting the vehicle, "but given the rest of the squad involved in Operation Splintered Skull were KIA, I don't feel much like celebrating."

"Understandable, son," Stafford went on, a large cigar poking below his gray mustache. "They all gave their lives so you could return with the intel. I'm assuming you all made duplicates and dispersed them among the convoy?"

"We did," he replied, producing a data-disc from the dashboard and handing it over. "Here's the Pulverizer schematics and blueprints, complete with flowcharts and data regarding their nuclear lasers. It took Matthews—God rest his soul—several minutes to breach their firewall, but thankfully, he was fluent in the Dul'ruak programming language. Not sure if you got a good look through your scopes, but it appears the warships are being manufactured with built-in deflector shields. If that's not bad enough, it appears the shields can re-direct our firepower to energy. Presumably, the info on the data-disc will give us a clue how to bring down these shields."

"Better yet, how to build our own," Stafford smiled, lighting up the cigar. "Sergeant?"

"Yes sir," yelled a random soldier who snapped to attention.

"Take these two down to the mess hall and make them whatever dinner they desire. They've earned it. We'll need them happy and relaxed for the debriefing tomorrow. The President's gonna wanna know what we're up against, and these two are to provide a first-hand summary of the Dul'ruak offensive and armament across the DMZ."

Kieran and Juan were ushered toward a bunker door. As they followed the sergeant toward the mess hall entrance, someone shouted, "*Hey!* Any advice for when we take the fight to them?"

"Yeah," Kieran smiled, before ducking into the bunker tunnel. "Watch your six! The Dul'ruak death rays pack a punch!"

SIM TRAP

BY

JULIAN MICHAEL CARVER

"You got it?" Robbie asked, beads of sweat dripping down his forehead.

"Yeah, chill, will you?" Marcel scowled, hands clenched around the precious artifact.

The historical item was a hand-crafted work of art; a twelfth century gold chalice, encrusted with an emerald rim dotted with rubies. The cup was so pure, Robbie could distinguish his sweaty scalp in the reflection.

Originally owned by King David I of Scotland, the cup had become one of the most noteworthy acquisitions of the museum back in 2033. Now it was 2122, and more coveted artifacts had been acquired. With a flood of new exhibitions, Robbie Bonham, a gift shop employee saddled with debt, was curious about where the item had gone.

More importantly, he wanted to know if it was somewhere convenient to burglarize.

When Robbie asked about the cup's disappearance, the chalice was rumored by the museum staff to have been privately purchased by Richard Wagner. Wagner was one of the senior-ranking board members and large shareholder of the museum.

Robbie didn't think much of it—until he was in desperate need of cash. As a gift-shop worker, the pay was hardly adequate. He decided a single cash windfall could change his life. Stealing the chalice could be that very windfall.

No sooner than he asked around about it, a woman working in the museum cafeteria confirmed the rumors. The Scottish chalice was purchased by the rich scumbag himself, Richard Wagner, for his private collection in his upstate mansion.

Having studied Wagner's schedule for weeks, Robbie knew exactly when the mansion would be empty—Tuesday evening. Of course, he had to break a couple things to make it look like a random burglary, not the organized endeavor it *really* was.

He would have stolen more from Wagner's mansion in the robbery, if not for Richard's numerous security measures. Many rooms were sealed off behind steel-barred door jams.

Robbie couldn't believe his luck. Coincidentally, the chalice was the only valuable item that wasn't sealed off. When he saw the golden cup, he couldn't believe his good fortune. He found it peculiar that Wagner would leave such a priceless treasure ahead of the protected vault.

But who cares! I'm rich!

"How do you plan on selling this off?" Marcel asked, snatching up the chalice with a leather-gloved hand. "As soon as this thing pops up on the inter-web, the cops will pounce."

"Black market, my friend," Robbie announced confidently as they shuffled out of the room. "It'll be a cinch, *really*—"

SHHHH-ZZZZZZZHHHHHHH!

A klaxon blared from unseen speakers. Robbie froze, fearing he tripped a hidden alarm tucked in the door jamb.

"*Whoa!*" Marcel cried. "What did you do?"

"*Jeez!*" Robbie gasped, faltering backward. "What's

happening?"

As they entered the next room, the walls began to spin. The doorway ahead moved away on its on own axis, independent of its apparent installed location. The bland wallpaper began to glitch and morph. Soon, the pattern projected an animated 3D rendered environment.

Marcel froze, mesmerized by the spiraling virtual world. Robbie turned to flee into the room they just left, only to be met with a baffling sight.

The doorway there was gone too, replaced by a world in motion. Struggling to decipher what he was looking at, Robbie noticed waves taking form; chaotic tidal waves in the middle of a stormy ocean. He looked up, discovering the roof transitioned from a white surface to a stormy sky, interspersed with rain and lightning. Waves washed at his feet, offering glimpses to the dim world below. Robbie could see shadows of whales and sharks swimming in the darkness.

"*Dude!*" Robbie exclaimed, doused in sweat. "I'm freaking out here, man! What is this?"

"Relax," Marcel said, more annoyed than alarmed. "It's only an *illusion* of a storm. It's meant to scare us. Initiated members of the Shadow Fang smugglers talked about these rooms. I think it's called a sim trap."

"A s*im trap*?"

"Yeah, a sim trap," Marcel said, handing Robbie the chalice. "Basically, a simulated mouse-trap designed for catching crooks like us. Rich socialites install these in their estates. The rooms are designed to look normal, but in reality, they are a motorized matrix of panoramic video screens. The room itself spins as the environment comes to life, offering no clue where the door is. The door is constructed with a video LCD, blending in with the panoramic environment. While the walls spin, the surfaces portray a single complex image. This confuses the viewer as to where the exit doors were to begin with. Looks like Mr. Wagner programmed his sim trap to display a stormy sea. Not a bad choice. The waves add confusion to which direction you were facing. Just looking at the simulation is disorienting."

"What do we do?" Robbie asked frantically. "I can't get caught, man. I'm already on several watch-lists for other petty crimes."

"Start feelin' around for a doorknob," Marcel guessed, running at the VR display. "We find the knob—we escape."

"Even if we *do* find it," Robbie continued, "Won't it be automatically locked?"

"Still, we might be able to kick it down."

"Hell, Marcel! I thought you were a top-class thief. You should've seen this comin'!"

"Shut up and feel the wall, I said!" Marcel snapped. "Or I'll deck you one!

"*Damn!*" Robbie whined, beads of sweat saturating his forehead. "This mission is a total disaster. How much time do we have?"

"I don't know, asshole! Sim traps trigger silent alarms. As we speak, cops are probably coming. When they get here, we better be ghosts!"

"Shit! Okay, I'm feeling! *I'm feelin'!*"

Robbie ran his hands over the tumultuous panoramic. Waves rolled as his palms met the screen, interacting with his touch while frothing into seawater. Amid the ebb and flow of the current and torrent of rain, Robbie finally clasped a doorknob.

"Marcel! Dude, I found it!"

Robbie flung the door open. Marcel ran up beside him. Ahead, the barred-off alcove beckoned—the chamber containing the empty stand previously supporting the chalice.

"Nice job, idiot," Marcel whined. "But this is the same room we just came from! We need to leave through the *other* room! The one with the estate entrance? I thought you were smarter, Bonham."

"Easy," Robbie smiled nervously at the jab. "Shouldn't it be right on the other side?"

"It *should* be," Marcel frowned, "But remember. The walls spun as the simulation started. The door could be anywhere. Translation: start feeling around, scumbag!

Unless you wanna be a permanent fixture in Wagner's museum of horrors."

Both men dove at the walls, sprawling out against the panoramic screen. Flashes of lightning zipped through the simulated sky. Tidal waves dispersed over the ceiling as if the thieves were sealed in a dome.

"Shit, Marcel!" Robbie whined. "I'm freakin' out here! This was one big mistake!"

"Cut it out, Bonham!" Marcel snapped, body-hugging the video wall. "Like it or not, we're stuck in this hamster ball together. Dammit, where is this handle?"

"I think I got it!" Robbie exclaimed, grabbing onto an object. "Yeah, here it *is*—"

"Watch it, idiot!" Marcel shrieked, reaching forward in terror. "*No!*"

Robbie went cold; a numbing sensation tingling his body.

The unthinkable happened. Amid his joy of grabbing the handle, he let the chalice slip from his hand. Effortlessly, the object fell from his fingertips, sinking to the chaotic waves at their feet. In a ringing reverberation, the cup struck the animated floor, shattering on impact. The shards skittered over the floor, dispersing across ocean water.

"You *idiot!*" Marcel shrieked. "That was our paycheck!"

"I...*I*..." Robbie struggled to form words, sinking to his knees.

Suddenly the storm ceased. Waves and rain faded back into bland wallpaper as the room reshuffled. Both doors flung back to their starting position. As the final door clicked into place, it was flung open from the outside.

"Oh, shit," Marcel uttered, staring in bewilderment.

Richard Wagner strode into the room, escorted by four police officers and a handful of wealthy socialites. Marcel backed up, as if there was any way out but the barred-off atrium in the next room. Robbie sat there on his knees, cradling the broken chalice. He was dumbfounded.

"Well, well, well, Mr. Bonham," Richard began, his curly mustache masking a haughty smile. "I thought I might've found you here eventually. You were a delightful test subject for my sim trap I had installed last year. Once I heard you were asking around about the chalice, I presumed you might be interested in acquiring it.. Given that I'm aware of your income, I figured you could by no means buy it outright. Therefore, I deduced you either really enjoyed looking at the chalice and missed it, or, more than likely, you meant to *steal* it. A little background check I ran on you was quite-telling. Several pick-pocket attempts in your high-school years. Grand-theft auto once or twice. Fingerprints on a few other shady spots where crimes were committed, investigated, but otherwise remained unsolved. But a heist like *this?* I must say, I didn't think you had it in you. And a word of advice, Mr. Bonham: Don't ask around for things like my house address to my staff. Most are quite loyal. I thought you were too. And to think, I was going to pay off your debt and give you a fat raise once you reached five years on the job. And that chalice was a glass decoy. You didn't think I'd let the real one out in the open, did you?"

Robbie stuttered incoherently, unable to form words. Two policeman hoisted him off the ground and cuffed his hands behind his back. Somewhere behind, Marcel made a move to run, but authorities apprehended him in quick order. Seconds later, he was cuffed in the same fashion.

"You kids would've gotten away with it too," Richard grinned, "If not for my meddling sim trap."

A few businessmen chuckled at the bad joke. The cops remained stern.

"Good one, chump," Marcel mouthed, carted off by the police.

As the policeman tugged Robbie through the doors past the other businessmen, Richard turned and called back.

"Oh, Mr. Bonham," he called mischievously. "You can thank me for giving you a decoy. Had you damaged the original, you'd owe me several million dollars."

TOOTH AND CLAW

BY

JULIAN MICHAEL CARVER

The first thing Rourke Silva felt after the environment reconstructed was the biting cold. Even through his insulated time-suit, he was unprepared for the temperature shift.

Gone were the technicians and dark warehouse. Instead, his view was replaced by an icy landscape, not a human in sight.

Eerie, he thought. *But I prefer to work alone. Less complications.*

Fighting off time delineation nausea common with time-jumps, Silva fell to his knees. Within seconds, data from the time-disc completed the transfer sequence. The entire event lasted less than a minute, as bit by bit, Silva was sent to Earth's past via tech from Yost Enterprises. The technology was relatively new; only a few decades old. With all the bugs worked out, time-travel had become an ideal resource for scientific study.

The only caveat—time-travelers had to swear an oath not to alter time in significant ways. Only small aspects of time-travel were permissible, such as harvesting artifacts, documenting or confirming historical events, and extracting DNA of extinct specimens.

Such was the operation of Yost Enterprises, a zoological preservation initiative with a single goal: the re-construction of the Pleistocene Epoch, to be erected on two hundred acres in northern Saskatchewan. The objectives of commissioned time-jumpers were simple—acquire DNA of extinct Ice Age fauna for these specimens to be brought back to life and flourish. Many of the larger, well-known creatures were already acquired through DNA—extinct horses, Columbian mammoths, and giant sloths.

When it came time to acquire the final DNA strand, Yost Enterprises wasted no time in employing the renowned talents of Rourke Silva.

Silva deemed himself the bravest jumper ever to activate a time-disc. He'd been in the midst of the Titanic sinking in 1912, in Pompeii when Vesuvius erupted in 79, and even Normandy during D-Day in 1944. Every time-jump he returned unscathed, completing missions for high-paying clientele.

When business mogul Joshua Yost, CEO of Yost Enterprises, hired him to successfully acquire smilodon DNA—also known as a saber-toothed tiger—Silva jumped at the opportunity and hefty paycheck.

Can't be any worse than the megalodon DNA mission, Silva thought, recalling when a marine institute contracted his skillset.

Getting his bearings, Silva studied the new surroundings.

The Pleistocene Epoch reminded him of a peaceful wintry forest. Snow hung to the *Darcycarpus carpenterii* trees from a recent storm, dotting the ground around the trunks. Boulders and rocky malformations protruded the slope, ascending to the terrain's summit fifty-meters up. The trees became more sparse until ending at the apex, where an outcropping of rock and snow awaited. It would be the perfect place for a cave.

And that's where I'll find ol' smiley himself, Silva

thought, preparing for his latest adventure. *I bet my ass there's a cave up there.*

First, he placed the time-loop disc on the ground. The riveted steel ring had been engineered to transfer him back to present-day Texas. If the time-loop was successful, it would send him to the exact spot he was standing now, where a Yost warehouse had been erected over the location of recovered smilodon fossils. Time-loops only operated correctly over the exact location where a jumper initialized the protocol. Thus, dropping the disc was the most crucial part of any time-travel attempt. If one failed to place the disc within reasonable distance from the portal, one may become stranded in the past, as a link to the future disc would be unattainable.

Second, he checked the weapons provided by Yost's associates. He was given a Vopp-branded tranquilizer-delivery weapon; a projectile launcher that administered enough cc's to knock out a hippo. Silva guessed it would be more than enough to neutralize a smilodon. Four darts remained tucked in a protective case, each with their own slot and surrounded with beveled foam. Silva retrieved one dart and slid it into the loading port before shouldering his gear.

The time-device will be active for an hour. That should be more than enough time to complete this job. Shit, Yost is paying so much for this, I should see what else I can recover while I'm here. Let's see. The fossils indicate the presence of smilodon right around this—

Two feet ahead, the first sign of his target appeared; a large feline track, caked in the muddy swath encircling a snow patch. As expected, the track led uphill toward the boulder cluster, where Silva anticipated the creature's den awaited.

Yost Enterprises conducted a study of the terrain a month prior, estimating where the creature's den would be. This information was based on recovered fossils in the vicinity of the warehouse. Finally, carbon-dating the rocks gave a rough estimate of when to set the time-loop. Silva judged from what he witnessed so far, the data was accurate.

Switching the safety off the tranquilizer, he proceeded up the embankment. The view was utterly astonishing. Droves of snow-laden conifers filled the valley beyond, nestled on hills like an idyllic painting. A frozen river skated between the valley some miles away, where a mammoth herd was grazing. Other mammals were playing on the cove, splashing in the shallows. Silva read through the debriefing on Pleistocene wildlife several times, but couldn't identify them. It was possible there were no traces of these animals in the fossil record, and thus no record of their existence to present-day mankind. As such, their DNA would likely be highly valuable—even priceless.

Perhaps a last-minute DNA extraction, he thought, shuffling up the hill. *No! Stick to the plan. If one of them happens to wander past the time-disc, then tranq' one and extract DNA. Right now, stay focused. Smilodon are expert hunters. They could be watching you this very minute. Remember the megalodon? Yeah. You don't want to underestimate extinct hunters. And in their own environment, they'll have the edge.*

He shivered in his time-suit, noting how much colder ancient Texas felt than its present day counterpart. After a short sprint, he reached the ancient boulders comprising the hill crest. Arriving at the first rock, he paused. Somewhere nearby was a killer; arguably the apex predator of the Pleistocene.

Careful, Rourke. Don't get cocky! Just extract the DNA and get back to the time-disc... Whoa! Here we are...

A chill crept up his spine. He had arrived at the destination.

Ahead, a cleft in the rocks beckoned. Grisly bones lined the entrance of the cave, bearing gnawed markings indicative of serrated fangs. Dried blood adorned the rocky facade like a collage of horrific cave paintings. The crevice was dark, giving little indication of the den's depth.

As Silva approached, a gentle rumble seeped out from the entrance; a feline whine.

I'm definitely in the right place!

The inside of the cave smelled like a toxic landfill. Rib cages, femur bones, and skull fragments lined the ground, illuminated by his helmet flashlight. There were fresh carcasses there too; some with fleshy organs and entrails. He breathed through his mouth to stop from vomiting. The air itself seemed heavy, as if the slaughtered creatures left a layer of film that hadn't dispersed.

Bingo!

Ahead, his prize appeared. A large figure tore into a mammal carcass, back-lit by a secondary entrance to the cave. It was as large as a grizzly bear, covered in matted orange fur with a central brown stripe running from its neck all the way to its tail. It was unmistakably feline and carnivorous, resembling a Bengal tiger without vibrant stripes. When Silva noticed the large set of serrated upper canine teeth, he confirmed his target. The creature was a smilodon.

The big cat pivoted on its hind legs, glimpsing the intruder. Leaping from the fresh kill, the creature moaned in irritation, scraping the cave floor with its claws. Silva observed the specimen was a mature female. He wasn't sure if that mattered for Yost's documentation, but he would make a note of it.

Easy, kitty...

Baring its large fangs, the creature let out a sinister roar as it charged—only to be met with Silva's tranquilizer dart.

The projectile hit the creature in the chest, sending the smilodon tumbling in a heap. The beast was out cold, completely unharmed.

That was too easy, he smiled, pulling out a syringe and a storage vial. *Now for a little prick and I'm back to the present. Stay still, Shere Khan. This won't hurt a bit!*

He bent down in front of the sleeping tigress, inserting the needle under the scapula. The smilodon flinched, but settled as blood seeped into his syringe. Silva dislodged the needle and deposited the contents into a vial. As he was screwing on the vial-cap, a shadow fell over the cave, followed by a deep, guttural growl.

Oh shit! The mate! Just like the megalodon. How do I

always forget about the damn mates?!

In terror, Silva spun to the secondary entrance of the cave. There, a large male smilodon sauntered through the entrance. The beast, a meter and a half tall, locked eyes with him. From its jaws, the beast dragged a herbivorous creature along the callous ground. Spotting the mysterious visitor standing over its mate, the smilodon released its kill, letting the carcass splatter onto stone. With a menacing growl, its eyes narrowed on Silva, fur ruffling in anticipation of tasting unfamiliar prey.

Shit! Oh hell...

The tranquilizer weapon lay discarded at his feet. Even if he moved fast enough, Silva knew the weapon was unloaded. A dart would need inserted if a defense could be mounted, and as long as that took, the smilodon would already be on him. The mission had suddenly become precarious. He counted himself lucky if he lived to tell about it.

"Easy," Silva declared, imagining how weak he looked. He placed the vial in his pocket, backing up cautiously. "Easy, tiger."

The male smilodon followed, creeping forward at a faster pace. The creature reached its unconscious mate, just as Silva arrived the front cave entrance. Nuzzling the unconscious female, the smilodon sniffed the wound from the dart. Its fur ruffling in anger, the large cat discovered where where the needle was jammed for DNA extraction. As he started away from the cave mouth—his gear left behind in the tunnel—the cat shot him a final glare. Then, face contorted into a primordial scowl, the beast leaped over its mate, bounding straight for Silva,

SHIT!

He turned to run, heart pounding through his time-suit. Sweat soaked his forehead, stinging as perspiration met with frigid air. He considered himself a fast runner. For a man in his mid-thirties, he kept up with an exercise regimen, a constant presence at the gym. In the line of work of time-jumping, athleticism was practically a requirement.

However, against a four-legged smilodon in its prime,

he knew the beast would effortlessly catch him. With his tranquilizer and ammunition back in the cave, all he had to survive were his instincts and a single utility knife wedged in a boot-holster.

The smilodon caught up with him halfway down the hill, equidistant from the time-disc and the cavern mouth. Anticipated being sacked from behind, Silva pivoted, reaching for his sheath where he kept the knife. He turned just in time to see the beast soaring at him, fangs barred in delight.

"*Ooo-f!*" he cried, rammed by the creature's weight and pent-up momentum.

As the saber-toothed tiger collided with him, he managed to draw the knife. The creature seemed undeterred by the weapon, moving in for a powerful bite. Swiftly, its powerful upper canine fangs flew at him. He threw his arm up to defend his throat. The smilodon latched onto his forearm.

Silva's scream was so loud and feral, he would've been ashamed if someone heard it. His time-suit was equipped with thin armor-lined sleeves, but the creature's bite-force was too powerful for the outfit's defenses.

He screamed again, feeling his forearm breaking apart. It had become more of a limp noodle more than a functioning appendage. The pain was unbearable. He fought the urge to blackout, knowing he wouldn't be around to wake up.

Bones splintering within wrist gauntlets, Silva was forced to drop the knife. The beast's head drew close to his own. He locked eyes with the primordial hunter, noting how the smilodon's pupils narrowed, relishing in his suffering. The cat's weight kept him pinned, but the slope offered a single advantage—a faint pull of gravity.

Silva kicked hard, moving both himself and the smilodon on top of him down the slope. The knife, discarded in the fray, was left behind. Now unarmed, he knew only one hope remained; getting to the time-disc and jumping to the present. Weary of turning his throat to his attacker, he glanced down the slope, then back to the smilodon.

The time disc was close, but could he wait that long? One arm was already useless. If his other arm went, his throat would be defenseless, and the death-struggle would be over.

Sliding on his back, Silva fought for his sanity. He wondered if it would be better to let the tiger slice his throat, ending his suffering.

No! Get the samples to Yost! You came here to do a job! Finish it!

The memory of his assigned task was all that fueled his will to survive.

As he kicked down the knoll, he heard a cracking of glass over the smilodon's roaring symphony; the DNA vial. In his pocket, the vial broke and fell out, joining the knife as another permanent artifact of the Pleistocene.

"Dammit! *Damn you!*"

Silva continued crawling.

His arm now a dangling appendage devoid of feeling and mobility, it served only as a weightless shield that the smilodon gnawed like a chew-toy. Effortlessly, the predator knocked his forearm aside. The time-suit sleeve in tatters, Silva saw the appendage was rendered to bone and a few strands of mangled muscle. As the creature went again for his throat, Silva offered his remaining functioning arm as a shield. The smilodon obliged, latching on. The cat crunched through the time-suit lining a second time, rag-dolling the appendage.

"*Auugh!*" he screamed, yearning for the nightmare to end.

Finally, his head struck a rounded, beveled surface.

The time-disc!

Just as the feeling was leaving his second arm, Silva hobbled over the cold rim, weighed down by the smilodon's bulk as the carnivore thrashed him. Worried the beast might throw him from the disc, Silva turned to initiate the delineation sequence—just as the smilodon lunged for his exposed shoulder.

"*AUGHH!*"

As the fangs sunk into his shoulder-blade, a blinding

aura commenced. The time-jump initialization protocol had begun. Suddenly the smilodon's bulk left him, relieving him of his suffering. Outside, the Pleistocene landscape began to brighten and pixelate. Geometry turned into crude polygons and mosaic forms. Space bled through trees, stars through grass, nebulas through the sky.

And then, confused but alive, Silva was whisked away.

"Get a gurney, *stat!*"

The doctor's voice was the first thing Silva heard.

His body was quickly reassembled through bits of data fizzling from the time-disc. As his senses returned, the first thing he felt was numbness in both arms, followed by immense pain that rippled shock-waves through his entire body.

As his figure was reconstructed in present-day Texas, he screamed involuntarily. Kicking off the time-disc, Silva found himself back in the Yost Enterprises warehouse. The male smilodon had vanished. As expected, the animal had been unable to transfer without a time-suit, leaving it stranded in the Pleistocene. He managed a smile, knowing the beast was long dead, collected by bone fragments in Yost's museum.

Medical staff rushed through the hedge of businessman and investors, hauling a wheeled gurney. Silva struggled to stand, unable to push up with both broken arms. As he was lifted from his side onto the gurney, his left arm flopped lazily onto his waist, rendered a mangled lasagna. The other arm might be salvageable, he thought, after extensive physical therapy. A gauze strip was placed over his neck as the gurney began to creak along, until a businessman with slicked hair—Joshua Yost—jumped in its path.

He held up up a single hand, ordering the medical team to halt while unsympathetic to Silva's critical condition.

"Sir, we need to get him to ER," urged a female nurse behind the gurney.

"Not without my deliverables," Yost barked, shielded by a pair of silver designer aviators. "Rourke, did you manage to procure a vial of smiley DNA? Forgive me for being blunt. My investment is on the line, after all."

"No," Silva replied, gurgling blood. "Fell out just before I time-jumped. Check my pocket. Some of it might have leaked out."

A pair of scientist rushed his pocket. After rummaging through, one shook his head.

"*Damn!*" Yost swore, slamming a cap-toe shoe to the tile.

"Wait a second," the other scientist announced, examining Silva's shoulder. "No kidding! Hey, boss! There's a tooth lodged in Mr. Silva's skin. Must've been deep enough that it was under the suit's deferential sensors, bypassing the transfer! Time may have allowed your DNA to travel right to us, Mr. Yost."

Yost rushed forward, looking at Silva's mangled shoulder.

"Son of a bitch," he remarked. "Is that a smilodon tooth, Mr. Silva?"

"Judging as how that's what nearly killed me," Silva replied, fighting to stay conscious. "I'd have to say it is, Sir. See, I told you I wouldn't let you down."

"Can you get DNA sample off that?" Yost asked his lead scientific advisor.

"Teeth are the preferred sources of DNA, Mr. Yost. So yes, this should work. Hold still, Rourke. Then we'll get you to ER."

The scientist reached forward with a pair of tweezers. Silva felt a slight pinch, followed by brief pain. Finally his muscle loosened. Although the pain in the arms insisted, his shoulder was relieved of discomfort. A second later, the scientist held a smilodon canine tooth in front of his face.

"Congratulations, Mr. Silva," the scientist smiled, examining the primordial tooth. "Mission accomplished."

LICENSE TO GLIDE

BY

JULIAN MICHAEL CARVER

"Watch it! Shift gears! *Drift!*"

"Sorry, Mr. Denning!"

Ricardo swerved the training glider, narrowly missing another hover-bike as he eased into the passing lane. The sky-ways over Medissa were packed, with gliders and hover vehicles of all makes and sizes congesting traffic.

He found that controlling a glider on a Sunday wasn't very hard at all; there were hardly any vehicles on the sky-way, offering plenty of reaction time for swift maneuvers. But on a Friday night, during the middle of rush hour, split-second decisions were the norm. He already had close calls with mid-air collisions, one of which caused his instructor to vomit out the window.

"Why on Earth did you choose this time-slot?" his instructor, Mr. Denning asked. "You must have a death wish."

"I didn't pick the time," Ricardo answered, anxiously swerving around a hover-motorist. "The written exam took *so* long. You know how hard the essay questions are. How ionic electrostatic propulsion works. Explaining Coulomb's inverse-square law. Not to mention; I'm terrible at multiple choice. By the time I finally submitted the written exam, there were so many other students lined up ahead of me for the gliding test. The fact that my slot timed out with rush hour was an accident."

"A word of advice," Mr. Denning started, his lanyard flapping around with each abrupt turn, "next time, just reschedule for a weekend test. Your chances of passing exceed greatly."

"How am I doing so far?" Ricardo asked nervously.

"*Uhm...*"

Mr. Denning looked down at his clipboard, lowering his glasses at the paper. Ricardo shot a discreet glance over, noticing how rampant the red pen had marked up the sheet.

"Take us back to the Department of Glider Vehicles," Mr. Denning advised, gripping a handle bar. "No need to proceed."

"But I haven't completed the three-point glide or a parallel swoop?" Ricardo asked, fearing the instructor's response.

"Unnecessary," Mr. Denning glared. "Back to the station, please."

"Yes, Sir," Ricardo swallowed. "I'm a little lost. Can you direct me?"

"This ramp ahead," Mr. Denning pointed to the right. "Ease over. You're good. Proceed down the ramp. The skyway forks ahead. Left at the fork."

Ricardo complied, dreading hearing his instructor's final remarks. Since departing the station, he was aware of several mistakes that drastically penalized his score; failing to turn signal, going too slow in the fast lane, and speeding through a yellow orb. He wasn't sure if flying to beat a red orb was a penalty deduction, but it certainly didn't help. The entire session was spent in tantalizing suspense, with Mr. Denning constantly swearing or looking fearfully in their rear view. Twice their glider had almost been clipped by passing vehicles before Ricardo swerved away, managing not to scratch the ship's chrome plating.

Denning complimented him for that; his only encouraging statement of the trip.

I totally bombed it, Ricardo thought as they coasted toward the D.G.V. sky-tower.

He dreaded rescheduling. For one, the test questions on the written exam would be randomized on the next attempt, forcing him to retake the first portion. Rescheduling would be a total nightmare; the wait periods were running two months out at the earliest. The worst part; he'd have to tell his friends how he had failed miserably at his first test, after bragging it would be easy.

I shouldn't care. None of them have their glider's license. Hell, they'll probably bomb it too!

"Middle hangar," Mr. Denning pointed. "Ease it into the docking bay beside the dispatch tower."

"Yes, Sir."

Grateful to have escaped rush hour traffic, Ricardo eased the glider into the area designated by Mr. Denning. In the windows beside the docking bay, he saw at least thirty other students eager to take the wheel.

Good luck with that, he thought, clicking the engine off as the glider parked. *They probably don't know rush hour just set in. Most will probably reschedule or chicken out.*

"Well," Ricardo began. "I take it the receptionist can help me reschedule?"

"No need to reschedule," Mr. Denning replied, scanning the paper. "You passed."

"I *what?*"

"You passed," Mr. Denning repeated himself, double checking his notes. "Ricardo, you're the first student I've had in five years to excel in rush hour sky-traffic. Usually the glider needs a new coat of paint with all the new scuff marks from student drivers that insist on this time slot. You made some mistakes and came close to failing, but you were masterful at navigating Medissa's sky-ways. That's a *first* in any student I've had. I expect these thirty-some students won't be as lucky as you, if they choose to proceed."

"You're not messin' with me?" Ricardo asked, beaming

with pride. "I *really* passed?"

"You *really* did," Mr. Denning smiled, dabbing his brow. "If you can drive rush hour in the sky-way, you can drive at *any* time. You made some mistakes, but not enough to fail. Your license will be printed in the reception area. But do me a favor. Tell dispatch to give me a ten-minute break. I need to take a migraine pill if I'm to do this thirty more times."

"Yes, Sir," Ricardo smiled, shaking the instructor's hand. "And thanks."

"Don't mention it," Mr. Denning said, relieved to exit the glider. "Welcome to the sky-way, son."

THE JUG

BY

JULIAN MICHAEL CARVER

"It's a jug," Odell gasped, staring in disbelief through digital binocular feed.

"A *what?*" Sarah asked, crouching behind the dunes.

"A jug," Odell added, jaw dropping at the surreal sight. "Remarkable. I haven't seen one in, oh, probably thirty years. I thought they'd all been disassembled and sold for scrap."

Two hundred meters down the slope against a wall of sedimentary cliffs, sat a centuries old carbon steel-plated WT-Mk. V water trawler. The vehicle, almost certainly on autopilot when last in operation, was wedged in a cleft. The tracks the vehicle left behind faded years ago with sand drifts. Odell surmised the vehicle had been stuck for several decades. Even from the distance, it appeared corroded with rust and faded by prolonged sunlight.

He managed a crooked smile through parched lips.

This far in the Rienna Dunes, there was a good chance the water trawler—or 'Jugs', as the old timers called them—remained free of pillage by marauders. Hopefully,

Odell thought, there would still be water in the tank.

"What's a jug?" Beckett asked, his throat dry and skin cracking.

"You two are too young to know about jugs," Odell chuckled, a sage of almost seventy years. "Back in my day before the Time of the Third Drought, communities across Daramis actually worked together. Trade routes ran throughout the dunes, fueled by communities engaged in commerce and exports. A common sight in the trade routes were Daramis issued WT-series mobile water trawlers. Most of us youngsters just called them 'jugs', because that's all they are; an artificially programmed trawler that hauls a large quantity of drinking water. They have internal compasses that up-linked their coordinates to satellites, dictating where they needed to travel. In the glory days of the Treadwell Dynasty, there were over five-hundred trawlers deployed, administering water to citizens all over Daramis. They were essential for providing water to desert mining operations. Jugs carry enough water for a hundred people, with enough room in the tank for at least a week."

"You sure it's not a mirage, ol' timer?" Beckett laughed, dry coughing while hiding from the sun under his cloak. "We've been out here a week. I've been seeing water everywhere."

For a twenty-seven year old, Beckett was in the worst shape of the three. Two hours earlier, he began to exhibit symptoms of delirium. Odell feared he may soon suffer heat stroke if they didn't find water or reach the end of the dunes.

"It's not a mirage if we all see it, Beckett," Odell replied, tossing the binoculars around his neck as he stood. "Mirages are different per person. We all see the same trawler. That's a *real* jug down there, and I'm willing to bet there's still water inside."

"What makes you so sure?" Sarah groaned, her nose scorched.

"I'm a man of fate," Odell stated. "We've been out here against all odds, making the trek only few have survived during the Time of Drought. This jug is the answer—a moving trawler we can ride containing enough water to last until we clear the wasteland."

"You can *ride* that thing?" Sarah asked.

"Not easily," Odell laughed, "but it's possible. I remember my father operating one through a small control console behind the front grill. If this jug has some juice, I may be able to salvage the controls and drive the rest of the way until the settlements."

"*Ugh,* don't joke with me, Odell," Sarah muttered. "I'm not in the mood."

"Come on," Odell laughed. "Let's go check it out."

The trio started down the slope, hoods draped to shield from blistering sunlight. Since the Time of the Third Drought, traveling through the dunes was deadly for wayfarers hoping for a shortcut to the Outer Daramis Settlements. For Odell and his company, there were no other options.

Marauders had ambushed their convoy on Sun Trail, scattering their group while pillaging their food and water. The brave ones stayed to fight, buying time for the elders and children to escape. Others were slaughtered onsite or while attempting to flee. Some escaped back to the green country, heading for the Daramis' capitol of Citauri.

Finding himself on the wrong side of the road during the ambush, Odell escaped to the sandy hills. Alone with only a plasma-flintlock rifle, he endured two days in the Rienna Dunes, refilling his canteen only once at a hidden oasis. On the same day, he encountered Sarah and Beckett; other survivors from the convoy who managed to escape.

Preparing to head North where the dunes transitioned to grassy country, their trek took a sinister turn. A band of a hundred marauders, armed with chemical-laser rifles and riding sand-beasts, were spotted through binocular vision. Fortunately, the marauder tribe was miles away, but their presence was enough to chart a new course. If the trio planned to reach the Outer Daramis Settlements, a longer route would have to be taken. With danger to the North and West, the next safest course was East—a grueling trek through sun-beaten dunes and rocky formations. The journey had been a risky one. If the heat didn't kill them, a dune lizard might.

As he lumbered toward the rusty jug, Odell couldn't help but smile. It was their first glimmer of hope since the convoy departed Citauri. Even if the jug wasn't capable of moving, it was a chance to fill their canteens. That alone was worth the hike down the hill.

"How have the marauders not pillaged this trawler?" Sarah asked a few steps behind. "It would probably give a tribe enough water for a week."

"Because even dune marauders won't come this far into the sand basin," Odell answered, reaching the base of the hill. "Dune lizards inhabit much of this territory. The lizards tend to hunt marauder sand-beasts. Since the Time of the Third Drought, the middle of the basin isn't used as an access route between Citauri and Outer Daramis Settlements. With the trade routes long gone, the marauders have no reason to trek this far out. It's a risk *even* to them."

"So you don't think they're following us?" Beckett croaked from behind. His voice was weak and posture clumsy.

"I guarantee it," he replied, approaching the cliff base. "Three stragglers going deeper into the dunes? Sounds hardly worth their time, especially when the convoy remnants fled into the green lands. It's ironic. Heading into the deadly heat wave might be what saves us."

Ahead, the jug grew close. At a height of seven meters tall and a length of ten meters long, the ancient, corroded vehicle was massive. Approaching the trawler from the rear, the jug looked free of indents or gashes; a promising outlook that there was still water inside.

Ten steps away at the base of the treads, Odell noticed something alarming.

Sand had been shuffled upward underneath the trawler, indicating an animal burrowed for shade. Only one animal made burrows that large in the dunes—the five-meter long carnivorous dune lizard, capable of killing humans with a bite full of alpha-neurotoxins.

Instinctively he threw a hand over his lips. Sarah

stopped in her tracks. Beckett lumbered forward, dizzy and only half-conscious.

"*Wha'*?" Beckett asked, glimpsing the ancient vehicle with a crooked gait.

"Signs of animal habitation," Odell warned, pointing to the vehicle's riveted treads half-buried in sand. "See how the sand's pushed out? There's even a few twigs around the base. A dune lizard was using the jug as shade and for nesting."

Beckett's jaw dropped. Sarah stared in defeat, her tattered hood whipping in the desert breeze.

"You're telling me there's a dune lizard right under *our* water source?" she asked.

"Possibly," Odell admitted, retrieving his plasma-flintlock. "You two wait here. If there is, I'm not sure we can proceed. These rifles are sufficient defense against marauders, but against armor-plated scales of a dune lizard, it may not be enough. I only have two shots."

"Make em' count, boss," Beckett muttered, slumping to his knees.

"Hang tight," Odell added, switching off the safety. He prepared to run. "Dune lizards can reach speeds of fifteen miles per hour. If I go down, you two can still make it. Follow your compass East, and you'll reach the edge of the wasteland."

"I doubt I'll make it another hour," Sarah swallowed, kneeling to help Beckett to his feet.

Odell turned toward the jug, raising the rifle while proceeding with caution.

"I haven't come this far just to be taken down by a single sand-snipper!"

Twigs and sand obscured his vision of the shadowed base, hiding what might be lurking beneath. Dune lizards were predators known for ambush attacks. They would leap from dens or rocky clefts toward unsuspecting prey, attacking at lightning speed. Delivering a toxic bite, death came swiftly for their unfortunate targets. The poisonous reptiles had been responsible for forty deaths in the past decade, at everywhere from Shadow Gulch to Diablo Pass.

Barrel pointed at the burrow meters away from the massive water canister, Odell jumped back in shock.

"*Aughh!*" he screamed, spinning away from the entrance.

"*What?*" Sarah screamed, hauling Beckett backward. "What?"

"It's dead," Odell uttered, shouldering the firearm.

He gagged while crumpling to his knees, face to the sand.

"*Augh*, smells like sand-beast shit! Probably died over a month ago."

"So we're in the clear?" Sarah asked, Beckett fighting to remain conscious against her shoulder.

"We're in the clear," he nodded, trying not to vomit. Sarah hurried over, with Beckett using her as a crutch. Odell peered under the jug.

Consumed by flies and maggots was the corpse of an adult dune lizard. The creature, nearly twelve feet long, was coiled in the center of the burrow. The flesh had been mostly eaten away, leaving muscle that stubbornly clung to bone. The skeleton looked brittle. The scales that remained were yellowed with age.

Probably got too old and croaked, Odell thought.

"*Ugh*, smells like death," Sarah breathed, slumping against vehicle. "Odell, I think Beckett's fainted. You have to... turn this thing *on...*"

"You don't look so hot yourself, kid," Odell observed.

He knelt to examine Sarah's forehead.

"I think you're ten minutes from passing out."

He turned to Beckett. Sarah laid him where the trawler met with the cliff—the only area of shade. His eyes were closed, face cracked into oblivion. Odell retrieved a canteen from his backpack, unscrewed the lid, and poured his last drops into Beckett's parched mouth.

"Do you... remember how to work that thing?" Sarah asked, slumped against the rusty hull, staring into space.

"I think so," Odell said, fumbling to the side panel.

A rusty spigot with a valve jutted out, accompanied by several buttons and levers. Hands gripping the rusted object, he cranked the valve hard to the right. With a loud squeal, the valve turned several inches, sprinkling flakes of rust to the ground. Odell cranked the valve harder, until the handle gave a final, laborious grunt.

Defeated, he fell to his knees, staring up at the dry rim of the spigot.

"Come on, *dammit!* Just give us a break! Just this *one* break."

To his right, he could feel Sarah turn to him. She had a gaunt stare, leaning carelessly against the jug hull. Her consciousness was beginning to wane.

"I take it... the water has dried up..."

"I'm...I'm sorry, Sarah," Odell groaned, his strength depleted. "I thought if we—"

He leaned forward, his throat dry. As he fought delirium, he couldn't form words to express his sorrow.

The sun cooking his shoulders, Odell fell forward. In doing so, the valve fell below his eye level, offering a different view of the burrow. In his dizzying spell, he saw the trawler's piping running from the valve under the hull, directly into the creature's tomb. There, he noticed something peculiar. The lizard's tail had bumped the piping. One of the vertebrae was wedged into an emergency shut-off valve at a junction to the water canister.

I'll be dammed!

Dropping flat on his face, he crawled forward. With renewed strength, he tunneled into the nauseating, putrid tomb. Vomiting from sun-baked smells of festering carcass, he kept his face down, careful not to scrape his back against the jug's rusty protrusions. Pushing the tail from his path, he thrust his right hand over the shut-off valve. With a hearty tug, the lever groaned. Finally, it released back to open position, allowing the flow to resume.

Yes!

The pipe whistled above him. Sounds of an ocean swell filled the tomb. Through the piping, he could hear fluid descending from the water canister, flowing through the jug until it reached the valve by his boot-heels.

Yes! Yes!

He felt a burst of pressurized water splashing from the outer valve, sending cold liquid washing over his ankles. He heard Sarah shout with joy, crawling to the spigot and placing her mouth under the downpour. Ten seconds later, she opened for a breath, just as Odell was back-shuffling from the crypt.

"Odell, you're a *genius!*" she screamed, cupping water with her hands and throwing it on Beckett's face. "It's *so* cold too!"

"Thank the solar-charged refrigerant cells for that," he replied, staring in awe at the waterfall.

Beckett awoke as Sarah splashed him again, delirious but refreshed by the touch of cold water. Sarah clasped his wrist, lugging him to the outpouring spigot. Odell waited for Beckett to finish before cupping a handful. Preserved inside the nano-crystal plated canister and cooled by solar-charged refrigerant cells, the old water was kept pure. He lowered his head over the spigot, allowing nearly half a gallon to spray down his parched throat.

Fluids replenished and thirst quenched, he let the others take another turn, hustling to the front of the jug.

In their heyday, jugs were primarily controlled with artificial intelligence, traveling wherever their software dictated. However, a large bench was installed behind the front grill. This allowed for a driver to engage a manual control override in case the trawler needed to reroute.

Odell recalled a childhood memory of his father driving a jug, remembering where the control pad was housed. He scanned the front console along the bench. There, a single handle awaited. He yanked the handle open, and out retracted a data pad.

"This interface still has juice!" Odell shouted, happily slamming a fist on the dash. "Gotta love old school Daramis engineering!"

Slipping into the sunlight, the data-pad glowed with an activate screen, running a list of automatic updates for code long obsolete.

Odell swiped across the update prompts and menu options before arriving at the driving controls. There, he found his first impression was correct; the jug was on autopilot when it crashed. Its last movements were logged to fifty-two years prior when the Time of Drought began. With the press of a button, the autopilot switched to manual.

A warning pop-up box blinked on the screen: *Valve Open. Shut before proceeding to drive WT-Mk. V water trawler. Temperature gauge active. Heat levels dangerously high—Stay hydrated.*

Rubbing his hands together, he leaped off the bench and headed back to the spigot. There, he found Sarah and Beckett beaming with smiles, ready to depart. Beside them, the trawler's engine rumbled happily somewhere under the base.

"You did it, Odell!" Beckett exclaimed, having returned to his lively self. "I never doubted you for a second. Do you know how to steer that thing?"

"Good enough to drive in a straight line, I suppose," Odell laughed. "Sarah, turn off the valve. We should reach the edge of the dunes within two days, I'm guessing, as the crow flies. If any of the convoy survived and reached the Outer Daramis Settlements, they'll enjoy what we're bringing. Something tells me, they may be a little thirsty."

DATASYNTH: TEARS OF THE MOTHERBOARD

BY

JULIAN MICHAEL CARVER

In the distant future, humanity has been completely eradicated by prolonged wars, pandemics, political upheaval and natural disasters. Now, shadows of the human world linger on in the race of clones called Synthetics, genetically identical to humans with adaptive learning via neurological links. Their human counterparts, now deceased for over a century, served as the hosts to this novel race of androids; a culture nearly identical to their creators if not for their internal microprocessors.

Alone without humanity to guide them, these Synthetics hail from a single city—DataSynth: the last semblance of mankind; a bastion for the remaining aspects of human culture. As another Great Reprogramming season approaches, a wave of depression hits the city, leading to riots, fear, and uncertainty.

Electrician-502 walked down the desolate highway, trying not to focus on the blue spires of DataSynth glistening on the horizon. It was among those sapphire columns that the clone population worked, slept, and—when permitted—made love. Built over the ruins of Washington D.C. a century earlier, DataSynth had become the pinnacle of cloning achievement. Constructing the metropolis had been a group effort on the part of every clone. Although the city was near completion, there was still much work to be done.

It was also where the Great Reprogramming took place; an event that became every Synthetic's worst nightmare.

Once a year, every clone had to pay taxes in the official currency of the Motherboard; DataCoin, register for the Census, and—the worst part—be reprogrammed for career reassignment.

The process was excruciatingly painful, conducted by replacing the microchip installed on the back of each Synthetic's head. The chips were programmed with skills and terminology needed for newly delegated tasks. The re-programming phase was ordered annually to keep the Synthetic population motivated, and to fulfill the decrees of Council of DataSynth.

For a century, the Council reigned over the Synthetics, comprised of the ten original prototypes made from the bodies of the last colony of humans. In their decaying human bodies, the Council members were kept alive by neurological electrode links, powered from the city's data spires. In their advanced age, constant maintenance was required to keep the Council alive so the city could be governed. This need for perpetual power led to the first Great Reprogramming fifty years earlier, with the objective to keep every Synthetic fresh and ready to work. According to the Council, frequent reprogramming would be needed if the Synthetics were to escape the same fate as their human predecessors.

Unfortunately, apart from immense pain during the implantation process, the operation came with a lengthy list of drawbacks.

Programming for the newly designated skill-set wasn't always simple for every Synthetic. Some clones had trouble adapting to their new careers. Mistakes would happen often, and with certain sectors like engineering or electrical, deadly accidents would follow. Hundreds of Synthetics had been killed over the decades for failing to adapt.

Another drawback was unhappiness and lack of fulfillment. Poor mental health was rampant among Synthetics that were delegated with new tasks. At often times, new trades were seen as a downgrade to prior careers. If a Synthetic landed a trade perceived poorly, a whole year would have to pass before a new career could be scouted, as per Council regulations.

Finally—and arguably the worst setback—memory loss.

With implanted microchips came implanted memories, and with the removal of one's microchip came a loss of memories. Regrettably, every clone sacrificed something during microchip expulsion. This caused pandemonium for romantic relationships in DataSynth, with most marriages crumbling within a year. Some marriages had to be traced within the network to confirm they were valid to begin with, since memory loss was prevalent even among database administrators.

Turning toward the guardrail, Electrician-502 noticed rusty vehicles pushed off the road a century earlier, during the final days of humanity. The cars were evidence of a flawed culture long extinct. In the time of Synthetics, there were no vehicles, neither in air, sea or ground. Vehicles allowed travel abroad. The Council emphasized centralization to one area—a single region of control where this fledgling culture could be observed. Thus, vehicles were deemed illegal and discarded during the First Decree of the Council, dated eighty years prior.

Were they better off than us? Electrician-502 thought of the humans. *Maybe in some ways. But we're here and they are not. Impossible to tell...*

The sound of a pebble skipping made him look ahead. Amid waves of heat distortion radiating from withered concrete, a figure emerged. Electrician-502 could tell it was a female, clad in a blue vest trimmed in white—customary for accountants. She was younger than he, probably in her mid-twenties, and very beautiful.

As she bled into view, he noticed a sack-bag slung over her left shoulder, crammed full of belongings. Wherever she was going, he guessed she didn't plan to return for several days.

"Hail the Council of DataSynth," he greeted her in the customary greeting of the capital.

He raised his right arm in a stoic wave.

The female paused, glancing up from her thin cloak.

"Hail to the four winds," she replied after a short pause. "Because that's where I'm headed, stranger."

"The four winds?" Electrician-502 asked. "I don't understand, Sister? You're *leaving?* Do you think it wise to leave the Motherboard? The Council does not forbid such an act, but if you run into trouble, you won't be permitted to return. You will be an outcast of DataSynth, left to forage in the broken world the humans left behind. The broken world we inherited and resolve to fix."

"Something happened today," the woman replied, ignoring his warning. "I went for my reprogramming, but the microchip wouldn't dislodge. My head-port apparently soldered the chip in place, due to overheated circuitry and daily wear. What the doctors called a fluke, I thought it was a modern miracle. My body must want me to stay this way. I took it as a sign. I'm meant to remain in this current state, whatever this artificial *state* is. I'm not meant to undergo another Great Reprogramming. None of us are."

"What did your microchip installer say?" Electrician-502 asked.

"They scheduled my neck-port and neurological link to be removed, refitted, and replaced," she admitted. "I can't undergo that procedure. I've heard a link refitting hurts a thousand times worse than the reprogramming procedure. You have to be conscious the entire time. I'm not putting myself through that torment. There must be more than this pre-programmed artificial life, Brother. There *has* to be."

"Where will you go?" Electrician-502 asked. "Other

than the Lesser Domiciles on the Outskirts, there's nowhere else to call home. Your accounting knowledge will be wasted. How will you survive without the protection of the Council or without the love of the Motherboard?"

"It'll be hard at first, the woman answered, "but in time, my life will be better. I'm sure if given the opportunity to forge my own path, I'll survive."

She looked at the piles of rusty vehicles stacked over the guardrail.

"Don't you ever wonder what life was like for them?" she asked. "Before their society imploded."

"Sometimes," he confessed, studying the scrapyard. "But remember, Sister. Humanity failed. Their infighting and susceptibility to viruses and war was their downfall. How can we be sure that their society was superior to our own?"

"We can't, Brother," she replied, proceeding past Electrician-502. "But in my dreams—the ones the Council hasn't robbed from me—I see the fate of our creation, DataSynth. In the end, our human instincts will prevail. We will turn on each other, as did our host predecessors. It's in our blood, Brother. Despite our best intentions as subservient androids, we are still *mostly* human. These events are already coming to pass. I'm sure you've seen it in DataSynth. There have been riots as of late. People are turning against the will of the Council, and few have already fled DataSynth. I don't know how many more Great Reprogrammings the Council thinks we can endure. I'm getting far from the city before history repeats itself, and society as we know it collapses. Somewhere else, with the Synthetics migrating with me, we will forge a new race."

She continued walking farther out, heading for the Outer Settlements.

Electrician-502 turned and watched her go before shouting, "What of your computerized parts? What if you get an internal virus as the Council warns? Your human organs won't be able to fight a cybernetic disease without updates from the Motherboard? Without the life-force bestowed by our mother, you'll die."

"Then die I will," she answered, not looking back. "At least I'll die a *single* death as the humans did, instead of passing away every year during the Reprogramming. With every microchip transfer, a little piece of my soul dies."

With that, she continued into the waves of heat distortion radiating off the pavement, not looking back. After a minute she was gone, vanishing around a bend that fed to the mountains.

Electrician-502 watched her go before turning back to DataSynth. There, the blue data spires awaited, as did a lifetime of a daily grind with a painful yearly reset.

Somehow, he thought, the sapphire spires had lost their wondrous luster.

Gritting his teeth, he turned back to the direction from which he arrived. Letting his tool bag fall to the concrete, he proceeded toward the mountains, never looking back.

CAT-LIKE REFLEXES

BY

JULIAN MICHAEL CARVER

Shar'Tak tightened his claws around the wheel of the Milean cruiser, veering the nose around another asteroid. Dorian tightened his hands around a cold handrail, gritting his teeth at the near miss.

"You're out of your *mind*!" Dorian exclaimed, staring wide-eyed at his Felion pilot. "I've had about all I can take."

"*What?*" Shar'Tak asked, claws rasping the wheel. "Never flown with a Felion before?"

"I've flown with Felions many of times," Dorian answered, "and thankfully, I've been fortunate enough to live to tell about it! But you're driving is *completely* idiotic—even for a Felion!"

"Pipe down and enjoy the ride," Shar'Tak replied, short on patience. "The Union is paying good money for your safe return. We couldn't take the main route I had in mind; too many patrols. Our only chance was the Crater Belt. I've flown through the Belt so many times I've lost count. Each time—not a scratch on the ship. You, however, are the first passenger that won't shut the hell up! Now, asteroid-dodging is an art form. If you keep distracting me, Mr. Alesso, you can wait below in the sub-storage compartment."

The Felion turned, brandishing a fierce scowl. Dorian cringed, noting the drawn-back orange ears and glinting fangs. Felions weren't known for excellent piloting skills, but they were renown for short tempers and reprimanding slashes.

And for having nine lives, Dorian thought. *Damn kittens are lucky. Maybe that's why we haven't died yet. Not for skill, just blind idiotic luck.*

"All right," Dorian nodded, avoiding the Felion's wrathful gaze. "Do your thing, Kitty."

"Shar'Tak is the name, human!" the pilot replied, turning back to the tumultuous cockpit view. "No Kittys! No Fuzzy-Wuzzys! And certainly—unless you want a swift bat to the eye—no Pussy-Cats!"

"Yes, absolutely," Dorian nodded. "Sorry, Shar'Tak."

"You wise-guys are all the same!" the Felion went on, arcing the Milean cruiser past a meteorite. "Especially when you enter witness protection. You think nothing can touch you. More importantly, you mafioso castaways think you can say anything, like you're still under Cardone's protection. Let me tell you something, Mr. Alesso! Your mafioso ties mean nothing to me, or anyone else for that matter. You've been excommunicated! The only thing anyone wants from you is your testimony and what's on that holo-clip. If there wasn't a hefty reward for your safe return to Enos IV, you would've met my claws light-years ago. The mob wants you, alive or dead. If the Galactic Union wasn't paying so much, I'd sooner throw you in the clink and deliver you to Cardone."

"You've made your point," Dorian assured the Felion, raising hands in surrender. "I've just never been this far our before, and certainly not in the dangerous Crater Belt.

"Well you're in good paws," Shar-Tak said, "As long as you don't piss me off."

The ship swerved left, obeying the Felion's jarring

method of steering. The cruiser conducted an elegant spin around a pair of asteroids. Ahead, through dotted swaths of oncoming space rocks, their destination awaited; the forested world of Enos IV. From this distance, the planet appeared angelic, bathed in a hazy green glow. Earth-like in every aspect, Enos IV was a world specializing in Galactic legal affairs. Prolific cases spanning multiple planets had been tried and settled in the Enos Judicial System. Dorian's case, involving intelligence on the mob hit of Earth Ambassador Todd Clemens, was scheduled for trial the following afternoon. He assumed the trial would go like clockwork, thanks to a surveillance holo-clip that Dorian safely planted in his luggage. The information on the holo-clip contained his legal immunity—his bargaining chip.

It also put a huge target on his back from the mob.

Evidently, Cardone was tipped off that Dorian was planning on betraying the crime family. In haste, Dorian made a copy of the holo-clip incriminating several key members affiliated with the now-famous assassination. Given that the clip had Victor's own voice and likeliness ordering the hit, he decided it wasn't so surprising when tails followed them through New York.

A few trench-coatsthat's nothing, Dorian recalled thinking.

He was well guarded. Twenty armed agents helped him off the subway. Unfortunately, Cardone didn't stop with a few alleyway stalkers.

It didn't take long to realize the mob wanted him whacked—badly. Departing from Earth had been a living nightmare. Grav-car chases through Manhattan. Rooftop snipers with hollow-point rounds. Detonators planted under overpasses. Insanity—all of it.

The Union bodyguards, clad in body armor impervious to most weapon-fire, found the cat-and-mouse game amusing. Dorian however, found it terrifying beyond comprehension.

Gone were the days of lavish comfort he found under Cardonne's protection. Now he was on the wrong side of the mob's wrath, earning the number one spot on Victor's personal hit-list.

Once the Union handed him over to Shar'Tak at the NY Spaceport, the turmoil followed into orbit. A detachment of Cardone-funded fighters gave hot pursuit for days. Shar'Tak did well to keep Cardone's forces at bay via the Milean cruisers' powerful ion thruster propulsion. Galactic Union fighters assisted, but Cardone's forces gradually picked them off.

With only a handful of fighters left and delayed from the dogfights, Shar'Tak gained considerable distance from danger. But in the emptiness of space, a secondary detachment of bounty-hunter ships found them, commencing a deadly chase. Only this time, no Union ships were around to provide covering fire.

The chase continued until Shar'Tak detoured into the Crater Belt, where even mob pilots weren't crazy enough to follow.

After the trial—if he lived that long—Dorian Alesso, a former made-member of the Cardone Crime Family, would spend the rest of his life in Galactic Witness Protection. He would be wanted by multiple crime families and cartels, shipped away to some back-world planet after the court apprehended the perpetrators. There he would live the remainder of his life in isolation; a thought he both dreaded and took solace in.

This might be the last person I'll ever associate with, Dorian mused about his companion. *Perhaps I should be more respectful. But then again, the cat is one lunatic pilot!*

Suddenly, a warning indicator flashed on Shar'Tak's console. A glowing orange blip appeared on the radar as the monitor spat information nested in a dialog tab. The Felion turned and grunted, reading the strange language. Assessing the signal, the pilot frantically operated several levers and knobs.

"What is it?" Dorian asked, hands clammy. He had already guessed the chilling answer.

"Let's just say Victor Cardone really wants you to fry," Shar'Tak scowled. "The radar detects an unmanned attack ship approaching; 'Devastator' Class. No origins are showing in diagnostics, but I can guess who sent it."

"A *Devastator* Class ship?" Dorian asked, staring in awe at the radar blip. "Never heard of it."

"It's essentially a suicide drone," Shar'Tak replied, activating the rear-facing secondary thrusters. "Very expensive to produce. I thought the Galactic Union pronounced their AI tracking systems too unpredictable and ceased manufacturing them. I guess Cardone's payroll goes higher than I thought."

"You can outrun it, right?" Dorian asked, unable to mask his fear.

"Outrun, *maybe,*" Shar'Tak frowned, activating the thrusters and propelling them forward. "Outgun, no."

"What weapons does that thing have?"

"Chemical-lasers and orbital missiles. Devastators pack a wallop."

"And what do we have?"

Shar'Tak didn't answer. Instead, he turned his tiger-like gaze to the glass. Rock after rock whisked past the cockpit, narrowly missing the ship's wings and elevons. On the radar, the blip grew close, cutting the distance between both ships to several miles in under a minute. The Devastator moved organically, turning on a dime to avoid calculated asteroid trajectories.

"Damn, it's fast," Dorian stated, activating a rear-facing holo-feed camera. "I can barely see it behind the asteroid field, but it's comin'. Tell me our ship is packin' heat?"

"This is a Milean Cruiser, Mr. Alesso. It's a prisoner escort ship, primarily used for detention and containment. Some planets use Milean Cruisers for supply transport for reserve armies. Hence, it has no armament."

"Are you *shittin'* me, Sha'Tak?" Dorian exclaimed, running his fingers anxiously through his slicked-back hair.

"*Be quiet,* human! Now, listen! Go down to the storage compartment and grab your luggage. Make sure your evidence is secure. There's only one way out of this now."

"*What?* You're gonna eject me in an escape pod?"

"If it comes to it. Just do as I say!"

"*Ugh!* Leave it to a Felion to fly a snitch without any firepower!"

As Dorian unbuckled his harness, the Devastator appeared through holo-feed. Arcing through an asteroid cluster, he noted the ship's sleek pyramidal structure. A pair of chemical laser canons were mounted to each wing, as were two orbital missiles ready for deployment. With a calculated turn, the ship avoided another asteroid, pressing onward with ion propulsion. Within seconds, the drone moved into attack position.

"It's on our six, Shar'Tak! It's within firing range!"

"I know it is, you Earthly *fool!* Get your holo-clip from storage, now!"

Dorian fled the cockpit, hauling himself toward the stairwell at the corridor's end. By the time he gripped the rail, the ship shook violently, sending him tumbling down the riveted stairs. Falling ten steps to the storage compartment, he regained his stance, dabbing blood from his forehead. He would have to wait to tend to his headache. There was a more important matter to attend to—retrieving the holo-clip.

Chemical laser blasts! That was a close one. The cat can barely fly, but I sure as hell hope he can dodge!

Hastily, Dorian observed where the Felion's storage remained in messy stacks. He grabbed his suitcase and dashed back up the stairs, feeling more vibrations from the Devastator's barrage.

When he returned to the cockpit, Shar'Tak was steering wildly. The Felion was entranced by the chaos, as if one with the ship. With blind luck, he avoided green tracer rounds zipping overhead, riddling oncoming asteroids.

Dorian took a seat and unzipped the bag. With a faint smile, he confirmed the holo-clip was intact in its protective sleeve.

"It's all right?" Shar'Tak asked, eyes focused on the oncoming asteroids.

"It's all right," Dorian answered. "But we won't be for long if you can't shake this drone."

On the rear holo-feed, Dorian saw the ship approaching quickly, coming within a hundred meters. Shar'Tak dodged another asteroid, narrowly avoiding the Devastator's storm of light bursts.

Suddenly, the laser fire stopped.

"What happened?" Dorian asked, checking the holo-feed. "It stopped firing on us. Is it letting us go?"

"Don't get cute," Shar'Tak grunted. "Its lasers overheated. Next it will deploy *the—*"

"Oh, *hell no!*" Dorian gasped, mesmerized by the holo-feed.

Directly on their six, the Devastator deployed its dual orbital missiles. In a flash, the seekers left the drone's wings, proceeding ahead in a cyclonic duet. Each rocket was fueled by smaller ion ports that weaved a ghostly blue haze in their wake. Dorian stared in awe at how fast they cut the distance to their ship.

"Comin' up on us, Shar'Tak!"

"I *see em'!*"

The missiles closed the gap between both ships, swerving with AI tracking intelligence through the asteroid shower. Shar'Tak listed the Milean Cruiser to the right of a large rock, then under another. When leveling out on the other side, he uttered a meow of shock; an oncoming hailstorm of smaller asteroids soared at them. The bombardment would be inescapable.

"Hang on, human! This may be it!"

"*It?* What do *you—*"

The ship was pummeled by rocky debris. Dorian's nails dug into Shar'Tak's leather seat, palms flush with the handles. Blood trickled from his lips as his teeth crunched his tongue. The cockpit shook violently as warning calculations erupted with damage reports. A second later, the jarring vibrations ceased.

Catching his breath, Dorian opened his eyes. The dash was aglow with abstract language and idiot-light symbols.

Miraculously, Shar'Tak's lunatic piloting maneuvers saved them yet again. None of the asteroids struck the cockpit glass, but they did damage the ship's elevons.

"*Whoa!*"

A blinding aura enveloped them, pushing the Milean cruiser forward. Chunks of asteroid pebbles shot past, rendered to small meteorites. The missiles, unable to avoid the wall of rocks, exploded on impact. The blast rang out like a shock-wave, launching Shar'Tak's ship farther into the rocky space.

"That's it!" Dorian exclaimed. "We're home free!"

"Not yet we aren't," Shar'Tak added, scrolling through the damage reports with his free paw.

"What do you mean? That thing's out of weapons, ain't it?"

"You didn't catch what I said earlier, did you, Earth-Walker?" Shar'Tak frowned. "It's a *suicide* drone. It has one final weapon—itself. It'll fly right into us, detonating on impact. Think of it like a flying Swiss army knife, but also a stick of dynamite chock full of nitroglycerin. That last wall of rocks really did a number on our thrusters and wings. We pulled it together, but we're leakin' fuel, unable to accelerate, and can't pull off those crazy turns you love so much. All that said, the Devastator will catch us in no time."

"There isn't anything *else* you can do?" Dorian asked, watching as the blip on the radar approached.

"Well I suppose there is one thing I could do," Shar'Tak admitted, rapidly clicking through sub-menu options. "That thing has a magnetic-tow for escape pod's and ejected capsules. I could eject you in my escape sphere right into the Devastator's tow port and turn you over to Cardone. At least then, I'd live to fly another day."

Dorian gasped, taken aback by the Felion's cruel words.

On the holo-feed, the Devastator approached, growing rapidly into view. On the radar, its estimated distance was less than fifty meters. Five seconds later, it was forty meters. Shar'Tak was right. The ship would kill them both, and that moment was fast approaching.

"You turn me over to the mob," Dorian glared, "Then *what?* You think anyone will hire you after this? You'll be ruined! Not to mention, turning me over with stall the case. Clemons will never get justice for the murder. Don't you know this is the galactic case of the century!"

"And you know plenty about murder, don't you, Dorian?" Shar'Tak laughed. "You being an affiliate of the Cardone Crime Family, I'm sure you've seen it all. You're a scumbag! Clemons will get his day, it just might take longer. You, on the other hand, will get off with your testimony. As far as I'm concerned, you deserve to fry too!"

"You traitorous, backstabbing pussy-cat!" Dorian snapped, leaping from his chair. "I know nothing of murder! I ran a small bookie operation and manufactured illegal liquor for Cardone. I hope they give you the electric-chair for this! Do you have any idea how big this case is? Do you have *any* idea what I've gone through to attain this holo-clip? You're throwing away the *biggest* legal trial the galaxy has ever seen!"

"Mr. Alesso."

"What, you turncoat?"

"I told you," Shar'Tak groaned, pulling a lever on the dashboard. "Don't call me pussy-cat!"

With an industrial groan, hidden emergency slider-doors sealed them inside the cockpit as the room flooded with pressurized oxygen. The Milean Cruiser tilted on an upward axis as weight left the vessel. In the rear-view, projectiles shot past the lens; crates, bags, food rations, and outdated industrial ship parts. The ejected debris soared into the asteroid field—right at the oncoming drone.

The Devastator tried to chart a safe path, bobbing its nose as its scanners detected the sudden obstacles. With such little reaction time, the programming was unable to calculate an emergency route. Trying to serve, it sailed right into a metal pipe.

"WHOA!"

The shock-wave was bright and turbulent. Dorian shielded his eyes as he felt Shar'Tak's paw slam him into the co-pilot seat. The detonation created a powerful aftershock, forcing the Milean Cruiser forward. The Felion fought to operate the faulty controls, recklessly steering to avoid asteroids.

Then, as Shar'Tak cleared one final rock, they arrived over Enos IV's exosphere, free of the Crater Belt.

Dorian studied the rear-view. Any evidence of the Devastator had been wiped away in the rocky ocean, save for a few pieces of drifting shrapnel.

The nightmare in space was finally over.

With no intercepting Cardone fighters ascending from Enos IV, Dorian leaned back, managing a smile.

"So," he said calmly, wiping away brow sweat with his forearm. "You were never going to turn me over? You were just trying to rattle me? For all that shit I said earlier, I take it?"

Shar'Tak smiled, fangs exposed through pursed lips.

"A deal's a deal," the Felion grinned. "The Galactic Union will pay way more for you than the mob would. I suppose your life is too valuable to be handed over to a couple of petty street-thugs."

"So you *don't* plan on ejecting me?"

"I didn't say that," Shar'Tak smiled again. "Take a look at our damage readings. One wing nearly severed and landing gear unable to engage. I should be able to get us close enough to Enos IV before we bail out. If you haven't experienced the joys of a Felion escape sphere yet, you're about to find out."

"Is that just like a normal escape pod, only rounder?" Dorian asked cautiously.

"You ever see a hamster ball?" Shar'Tak chuckled. "I don't suppose you can picture free-falling from outer space in one? Don't worry, you'll have me to keep you company. Just watch out for my claws. With how unpredictable falling from the stratosphere is, I tend to fall out of my harness a lot. Prepare for a bumpy landing, Mr. Alesso!"

LAG TIME

BY

JULIAN MICHAEL CARVER

Initializing Simulated Home Reno V2.0...
Loading texture maps...
Applying Plugins...
Rendering Environment...
Commencing simulation...

This is my two hundred and twenty-eighth try, or should I say, failed escape attempt.

I open my avatar's eyes, glimpsing the same vision I've seen over and over again.; a single skylight, letting in the rays of the afternoon sun through the branches of a 3D Japanese maple tree. Two hundred simulations ago, I admired the computer's rendition of an idyllic Southern California afternoon. Now I just want the corrupted simulation to end—more than *anything* in my entire life.

As soon as the correct physics settings apply to my avatar, I leap out of the simulator chair.

I'm in my home, but not my *real* home. Instead, it's an artificial environment created through projection mapping;

a mock-up vision for my renovated property I've spent the last five years planning.

This morning, or maybe yesterday morning—I've lost track—something went horribly wrong in the software. The host terminal for the VR port located on the second floor of my old Victorian home had glitched, restarting my simulation every minute. Trapped in an endless loop of a low resolution 3D nightmare, the program keeps spawning me on the first floor of my house. Here, my real body remains strapped into the simulator seat. Unable to move due to a VR packet-filter override, I'm forced to rely on the virtual avatar to end my time spent in the sim world.

Why I wouldn't put the simulator chair right beside the VR access terminal? I'll never know, but my lack of foresight has bit me in the ass two hundred and twenty-seven times.

Unfortunately, the starting placement of my avatar allots only a minute to get to the second floor and reboot the system; a feat that may be possible for Olympic runners, but almost unfathomable for the glitching avatar that I'm operating.

You see, with a faulty terminal plagued with insufferable lag time, the deck is heavily stacked against me.

Over the past two hundred and twenty-seven attempts at reaching the monitor, I know what's waiting for me if I fail. The system will spawn my avatar back at the start of the projected environment at the simulator seat, leaving me marooned in this digital world until I reboot. With each failed attempt, I lose a piece of my sanity. For this attempt—my two hundred and twenty-eighth, if I failed to mention—my strategy is simple; *run!*

I take off through the lower floor of the house, watching as my view-port carries me down the remodeled hallway. There are 8-bit sconce light fixtures, pixelated varnished flooring planks, and bump-mapped beveled trim. At one point, I was impressed by the computer's calculations of my future mansion. Now, I care not for the pleasantries of this artificial world.

All that matters is a reboot; a hard reset to an outdated

machine I'll never again utilize. When I did escape the simulation—whenever that may be—I vowed to take a baseball bat to the server tower.

Clumsily I fumble to the bottom of the stairwell and begin my reckless ascent, bumping into walls as the texture maps glitch on impact. The environment streaks past as I bound three steps at a time, falling on the top step before I manage to tilt the avatar upright.

Move! Move faster, damn you!

The upper hallway feeds to my office, located at the end of the hall nestled into one of the home's decorative Gothic turrets. Knocking over hall furniture and breaking digital vases, I arrive at the threshold to my office.

Here, I'm greeted by the same maddening sight.

In the corner sits the VR simulator modem and the terminal control port. On the monitor, a dialog box pops up with an error message; the same error message I see every time I'm fortunate enough to make it this far.

The error message that makes me want to blow my damn brains out!

ERROR: Not enough memory in cache to continue Simulated Home Reno V2.0. Purge all memory on disk cache? Y/N? Rescanning for memory in ten seconds...

No!

*Know*ing the stakes, I bolt for the terminal. If the system conducts a full re-scan again, I'll be thrown back to the spawn position. Only a full system purge will be able to correct the mistake and free me from this looping hell-hole.

My mind is nearing the breaking point. Every time I fail is a soul-crushing defeat. If this cyclical calamity continues, the only hope for my survival is when the maid comes next Tuesday, but that won't be for another week. And in a week, I know that my real body—which remains downstairs and strapped to the sim seat—will be long dead without water or nourishment.

My avatar flies at the VR workstation: a terminal specially coded to mimic and operate its counterpart workstation that exists in the real world. With the dialog box checked for avatar override, and a cache glitch anomaly plaguing the software, my body is trapped in this maze of infinite insanity.

The only hope lies in piloting the avatar to purge the cache.

I can see the screen coming clear as my view-port nears its destination. A pixelated hand rises from the first-person perspective as I prepare to interact with the digital keyboard and then...

Shit!

Edges of the frame shift to low-resolution, fighting to display the moving virtual world and keep calculating for rendering my character's motion blur. Fighting the lag, the computer throws me forward, placing me just beside the workbench. In the sim seat downstairs, I can feel my body sweating as I frantically swerve the avatar to the left, bringing my view port within inches of the keyboard. In a flash, the computer lags again, making me overshoot the keyboard and placing me right in front of the terminal screen.

I look down in terror, seeing that one second remains on the screen until the cryptic restart—the restart that is prolonging this rendered purgatory and forbidding my departure. I reach forward, hand stalling in the frozen lag.

I glitch forward, hand grabbing the mouse and...

...

..

.

Initializing Simulated Home Reno V2.0...
Rendering Environment...
Loading texture maps...
Applying Plugins...
Commencing simulation...

This is my two hundred and twenty-ninth try.

DEATH DIVE

BY

JULIAN MICHAEL CARVER

Snorkeling in a commercial-grade, test-dive aquarium within a controlled environment; that's a piece of cake. Being submerged a hundred meters down in the abyss of an alien sea; that's something else.

These were the cryptic thoughts of Tad Baron as he descended the flowline of the Energy Earth Corporation rig, located on the Artieus Sea of the planet Okeanos. On this delightfully treacherous evening, Tad was terrified to learn a storm rolled in over the precise coordinates of the rig, delivering a maelstrom of roiling waves and hurricane force winds. To make matters worse, his view of more than ten meters away was a blur of shredded plankton. The lights from his atmospheric diving suit did little to improve visibility, and in the vast dark netherworld of the Artieus Sea, eyesight was the key to success—and survival.

Next time there's a crisis, he thought as he gripped the flowline, *I'm letting someone else volunteer for the suicide mission!*

Inside the single-person atmospheric suit, the tension

was palpable. Every meter down represented another step away from sanctuary, and another step closer to what lurked beneath. Deep-sea divers knew the risks well when they were contracted by the Energy Earth Corporation. Ordinarily, engineers had an entire contingent of naval operatives, armed with spear-guns and attack submersibles, to assist in deep-sea operations. Occasionally, armed escorts wouldn't be readily available for deployment, for one reason or another.

Tad Baron found himself in one of these precarious scenarios, and had only himself to thank for it.

On that particular day, all armed divers were stationed at other rigs scattered across the Artieus Sea. Earlier, this wouldn't have been a problem. There were no drilling objectives or diving operations scheduled for the day, so there was no reason to dispatch naval support.

The day went like clockwork, and he spent most of it above deck doing maintenance checks on rig equipment. That all changed around three o'clock in the afternoon, when the unthinkable happened—at the worst possible time.

Somehow down in the gloomy void, an oil valve opened to an faulty underwater spigot, spewing the valuable fluid into the tide. With the stakes high and the E.E.C.'s investment flowing away in the current, someone had to go down and stop the bleeding. This meant a daunting dive to the valve, located where the pile-secured template met with the seafloor.

You might say it's the perfect storm, Tad thought, trying out bad puns to cope with the terrifying nightmare.

Needless to say, it didn't work.

He bit down on his lip, watching through the oblong view port as the nautical world swirled around him, a blob of green, brown, and black. Above, the submerged lights of the rig sub-floor began to fade, masked by the frothing riptide. The waters of the Artieus Sea were a treacherous place, and not only because of the flash-storms.

A diverse array of aquatic fauna inhabited the vast oceans of Okeanos. Everything from microscopic algae to fifty-meter long whales had been spotted when the Energy Earth Corporation touched down. In the early years of sub-aquatic exploration to alien worlds, new species were discovered almost daily. Research had been conducted by the most astute marine biologists, who poured through hours of diver footage to study, categorize, and log the numerous novel species.

It didn't take long to pinpoint the universal trait common among Okeanos sea-dwelling fauna—unrelenting aggression.

Numerous scientific names of carnivorous species flashed through Tad's mind as he descended.

Deep-Water Gulper. Trench Shark. Mammoth Crab.

Almost all the species he could think of were bigger than himself, and as such, he assumed they were capable of *killing* him. He tried to spin the situation for the positive, imagining the amount of street-cred he'd accrue for being the only volunteer willing to brave the stormy sea.

The events proceeding the treacherous scenario were a blur.

An hour earlier, he was standing in the operations bridge of the rig. Sam Norton, lead drilling contractor of the operation, glanced the twenty divers over. A look of sheer disgust crept across his wrinkled brow as lightning flashed in the distance. It was the usual unpleasant scowl Tad grew so tired of seeing.

"I don't believe what I'm lookin' at!" began the inevitable tirade. "A bunch of scaredy-ass mamma's boys. I don't know what Treadwell is paying you grunts, but it's *way* too much. The E.E.C.'s already lost several hundred million from that spill. Every second we wait, that's precious oil flowing into the Artieus Sea and not in *your* bank account. Now if one of you shit-heads won't step up, suit up, and swim down there, I'll just have to nominate someone. How about you, Saunders?"

"Not me, Sir, please," Saunders begged, a twenty-year-old from Wyoming. "I got a kid back home, Sir. I'll gladly go down when the navy divers come back, but not now."

"*Pathetic,*" Norton spat as the ocean waves roiled

behind the glass wall. "You just earned a week of deck-swab duty, congratulations! You, Nichols. How's about it?"

"I don't feel like dying today, Sir," the brash New Yorker answered, "and with all-due respect, Treadwell hasn't been in an Okeanos maelstrom like *we* have. I've seen the teeth on those guppies real close. If there wasn't a naval escort, I would've been fish-food months ago."

"I thought New Yorkers were supposed to be tough," Norton grumbled, prodding Nichols square in the chest.

"Tough, indeed," Nichols replied, locking eyes with his boss. "Just not stupid, Sir."

The counter-comment sent Norton spinning in fury, slamming an crunched fist against a system console. When he finally composed himself, he stood with purpose, running both hands through his few remaining gray hairs.

"Look," he went on, "you're all makin' this entire operation look bad, not to mention, *me* look bad! Treadwell has called me personally and cussed me up and down the street. Every second that leaky valve is spewing oil is another layoff waitin' to happen. You all know what you're being paid to be here. E.E.C. is very generous in their salaried positions. High salary always comes with strings attached. You either have the balls needed to do the job or you don't. Just a bunch of *weak*—"

"Enough already," Tad moaned, taking a step forward. "I'll do it. I'll shut the valve off."

The room grew quiet. Tad felt all the eyes shift in his direction, as if he'd just volunteered to test drive an electric chair.

"What's *this?*" Norton smiled, gesturing in triumph to Tad. "Finally, a diver worth his salt! Listen, Baron, you go down there and get that valve shut off, and there will be a cheeseburger waitin' for you when you get back. I'll wake Dustin and tell him to grill you one. Not to mention a side of burnt fries. Don't think I've forgotten how you like em'!"

"For what I'm doing, Sir," Tad replied, "I'd also like a glass of that scotch you keep over your desk. Just like Nichols, I've seen guppie teeth close up. Mammoth crab pincers right in my face. With that storm out there, I'll never see anything comin'. You know how predatory species sightings increase in storms. It must rile em' up, Sir."

Norton nodded, folding his arms.

"You got guts, son," he grunted. "but a deal's a deal! One cheeseburger, a side of burnt fries, and a glass of 2403 Bollinger scotch in exchange for a little night swim."

That's all? Tad fumed, using his hands to propel farther down the flowline. *That's all I asked for? Hell, after this, you bet your sweet ass I'm calling Treadwell himself and asking for a ten-thousand increase! If he's really losing millions by the hour, I think he can afford it. And this better be the best damn cheeseburger ever grilled!*

Fortunately, he was well suited for the descent, given the newest suit developed by U.S. submersible developer Aquarius. His variant, the Aquarius Mk. VI Abyssal Diver, was a custom-fitted atmospheric one-manned submersible. With two shoulder mounted lights and swim-assist foot thrusters, the Mk. VI became a favorite for Okeanos missions. Improvements were made to the holographic HUD, including a depth gauge with an accurate reading of up to one thousand meters. As with all Aquarius atmospheric suits, careful consideration was paid to balanced internal pressure, allowing for rapid descents without risk of nitrogen narcosis. Tad appreciated the increased flexibility in the suit over the Mk. V, allowing for more versatile movements via articulated aluminum joints.

It wasn't until twenty meters down that he realized a single flaw in his particular suit; someone on the oil rig slapped a hastily-scribbled note on the radio system— *Broken.* Tad didn't appreciate the gravity of the note until he tried to communicate with the rig operations bridge. His microphone wouldn't power on, and no voices came through the speakers.

Any trouble he'd run into, Tad feared, he'd be on his own.

Above, the light from the rig began to wane, leaving him to descend deeper with only the glow of the shoulder-mounted flashlights for guidance. Traces from the oil spilling forth from the valve were evident, clouding his vision. Slowly, he was nearing his destination. According to his depth gauge reading inside his visor, he had a hundred meters before hitting the seafloor. Tad speculated that, with his luck, the valve would be at the very bottom.

Just keep climbing, Baron! Don't make it a big deal. Get down, turn the valve off, and get back to the rig. The longer you drag this out, the mor—

In front of his helmet, movement stirred in the dark tide. Baron paused, trying to regulate his rapidly beating heart.

Cautiously, the shape slithered toward him, coming within meters of his visor. A second later, the shape coalesced into the form of a yellow-fin saw-back bass. The saw-back was a unique species native to the Artieus Sea; a scavenger barely a foot long. Seeing a yellow-finned specimen was extraordinarily rare. Typically, they kept to the lower parts of the seabed, hidden among reefs.

If saw-backs are being coaxed to the surface, Tad thought, *I'd hate to think about what else the storm drudged up.*

The creature eyed him through the helmet, exposing its small razor canine teeth and amber eyes. It was infatuated by his movements, swaying to remain at eye level. Cautiously, it gave a lurch forward. Tad jumped, scaring the fish back into the column of diluted oil.

Jeez, even the little fish have sac.

With the curious fish having departed, he continued his descent, ignoring the many shadows circling behind the oily veil.

Looking at them won't make them go away, dumbass. If you sit and gawk at them, they might take it as a challenge.

He checked the depth gauge. Fifty meters to the seafloor, and still no sign of the problematic valve.

This was the right flowline, wasn't it? Shit. Any day now, please!

Wrestling with fear, he pictured his colleagues above in the rig, safe and sound on the deck and watching the cameras in awe, jealousy, and resentment until he descended beyond their view. Since his tenure employed by the Energy Earth Corporation, he had never made such a brash decision. Deep sea diving had usually been supervised by a flotilla of navy divers, keeping the aquatic wildlife at bay. Sure, every once in awhile a reef shark got cute, but it was nothing a speargun couldn't solve. Without cover of other armed naval operatives, diving on Okeanos was risky business.

Maybe the oil's keeping the bigger fish at bay...

He didn't know if the oil was helping ward off the predatory species, but the dark cloud certainly wasn't beneficial to his eyesight.

Forty meters. How haven't I hit this damn valve yet?!

All traces of green ocean were gone. Now in the thick smog of the oil cloud and far below the lights of the rig, Tad found himself trusting his instincts, feeling along the pipe for any signs of the elusive valve. Blackness surrounded him from all sides. He could feel the hairs on his neck prickling up, terrified of what might be lurking just beyond the black haze.

I have to be getting close now! It's so dark, and the oil will rise. Once the valve is found, I'll get my visibility back, but where is it? Where? Where—

Oil flew at his helmet in a torrent of bubbles, obscuring any view of the flowline only inches away. Hands clenching something industrial and round, half of Tad's vision returned in a flash. When his helmet found the edge of the oil cloud, he knew it was the open valve. The sea floor was close, lit from below by underwater lights controlled from the rig's circuit.

Finally! I knew the bloody thing would be way down here. It's about time!

He cranked down on the valve, pushing with all his strength to the right. To his bewilderment, the valve wouldn't move. It was already sealed off.

What the hell?

His hands drifted a few inches up on the pipe. Moving the helmet out of the smog cloud, he saw the valve had never opened. Instead, the oil spewed from a fault in the flow-line, inches above the valve spigot. The slash, no more than four inches in width, was gushing oil like a smoke cloud. Tad inspected the abrasion, noting it must have been something of tremendous strength to pierce carbon-steel plated piping.

This is beyond my pay-grade, he thought, staring in confusion at the fault. *They'll have to send a repair crew do—*

Lights from the sea-floor flickered, rotated, and then moved. Green light photons danced off his helmet visor, distracting him from the mysterious fault.

Damn storm's been affecting everything from the circuitry to the power lines.

Tad hung onto the pipe and looked down anticipating an electrical surge that was affecting the lighting grid. Below the lights were swirling, before moving into a coil while ascending to meet him.

Suddenly, Tad knew it wasn't rig lights, but something far more sinister.

The creature was a massive, slithering eel, aglow in green and yellow bioluminescence from luciferin-enzymes. The sea-serpent, over twenty meters long, brandished dagger-like, protruding teeth. Tad took note of the eel's mouth as it approached, observing the jawline comprised of bone-like plate incisors, perfect for puncturing a durable flowline. Its face—a hideous mangled visage—flew at his visor, opening its jaws to inflict its immense bite-force.

What the hell are you?!

Tad climbed upward on the flowline as the strange species snaked toward him. It was unlike any creature within the registered E.E.C. database of known marine fauna, and certainly wasn't listed on the Okeanos endangered species list. No sailor had made mention of bioluminescent eels, or any eels for that matter. It was a creation of his darkest nightmares; an emissary from the abyss, and undoubtedly the reason for the oil mishap.

In a backward frenzy, Tad propelled himself into the black veil of oil. Outside the smoky film, he saw the eel slither around the rig column, making a bee-line directly for the bubbles shooting from his oxygen tank. Suddenly at the last minute, it darted off course, avoiding the oily glaze that Tad had shielded himself in.

He could hardly believe it.

The creature, whatever it was, had caused the punctured flowline, yet was repulsed by the presence of oil. Coiling in anger, the eel commenced a second charge, rearing up several meters before spiraling around, launching like a torpedo toward Tad's position in the oil geyser. Again, as if on queue, the creature paused at the edge of the black film, before retreating once more.

Unbelievable. This sea snake is tryna' take me out!

Floating on the current just a few meters outside the pipe, the eel centered its attention on Tad, studying the scenario, weighing the odds of success. Now up close, he glimpsed the true size of the deep ocean predator, bathed in self-illuminating light that made it as beautiful as it was deadly. The animal's back was lined with barbed quills; a formidable defense against ocean predators. Coupled with the creature's long jagged teeth that protruded outward like fishhooks, the eel may have been the planet's deadliest aquatic predator.

Too bad I don't plan on sticking around to admire you!

Wasting no time, Tad began to yank himself back up the pipe. Like a magnet, the eel followed him at the same altitude. Strange hypnotic glowing patterns began to emerge from the eel's belly, firing a dazzling light show of concentric circles across its serpentine frame. A cat and mouse game ensued as the eel switched positions, altering its course to the other side of the pipeline while making certain to avoid the oil.

Maybe if you didn't chomp our flowline, you could've eaten me by now, Tad glared, moving a few meters higher.

As he continued to ascend, a sickening feeling welled in his gut. Abruptly he stopped, swallowing the grim reality.

Once I clear the bulk of the oil cloud, the eel might feel secure and confident enough to attack...

The fear had merit. Thus far, the creature was kept

at bay by the oil spill. But once the oil began to disperse closer to the surface and dilute on the ocean current, he wouldn't have that safety net. And without naval divers or a spear gun, he would be a sitting duck.

Tad looked from the glowing eel back to the surface. Lights of the rig sub-floor were barely visible through the murky ocean. The depth gauge revealed a height of fifty meters. Hugging the flowline, Tad wagered he may have another thirty meters of safety within the oil spill. After that, when the oil became diluted with ocean water, he gave himself a fifty-fifty chance. Swallowing his fear, he resumed the ascent, dreading every step closer to where the water grew clear.

To his left, the eel drifted closer to the dark veil. Tad switched sides, keeping the pipe between himself and the incandescent serpent.

You son of a bitch! You just can't let me go, can you?

Despite its deadly nature, Tad couldn't help but marvel at his admirer.

The eel was a remarkable creature; a living example of otherworldly nature gone horribly wrong—or dangerously, beautifully right. It represented to Tad the entire problem with the Treadwell operation on Okeanos—radiant riches in the face of uncertainty and gloom. It was a metaphor for his entire tenure on the Artieus Sea.

Dangling money in the face of young divers, yet not explaining it may come at the price of their lives. Treadwell, you son of a bitch. If I make it out of here, I'm giving you hell!

The depth gauge relayed a reading of forty meters. Lights from the rig became clearer. The oil cloud began to spread, coalescing with ocean water. Outside the black film, the carnivorous eel slithered closer, retreating when coming into contact with thinning oil particles. Tad could feel his heart beating through the suit, his brain fighting a headache, his bowels giving out of sheer terror as the eel's grotesque details became clear.

Had he seen the strange creature on a data-pad feed, he might have enjoyed its surreal beauty and cunning wisdom.

But in the darkness of the Artieus Sea, all he could do was pray his death would be quick.

Thirty-five meters.

Tad climbed. He could feel his lips bleeding in the helmet, his canine teeth grinding down into the epidermis.

And to think, I came that close.

In seconds, the oil faded into ocean current.

Time had run out.

Come on, you ugly bastard. I know you want me!

With the smoke cloud diminished, as expected, the glowing eel charged, jaws agape. Unable to stop the creature's imminent charge, the only thing Tad could do was pivot backward, spiraling around the pipe and using it as a barrier. With a powerful undertow, the eel launched past, missing his suit by inches while chomping water. With the creature coiling around and preparing another pass, he pivoted on the pole, shimmying up a few more meters.

The monster eel followed.

Bubbles flaring from its mouth like a fire-breathing dragon, the creature lunged again. Tad swung back around, allowing the serpent's powerful riptide to blow past once more, its force so great it almost sucked him from the flowline like a tornado. His fingers tightening around the pipe, Tad climbed another few meters skyward. The lights from the rig were coming into focus, but were still a considerable distance away.

By the time he looked back to the surrounding sea, he could feel goosebumps prickling his arms.

The mysterious eel no longer stalked him from the sides—but from *below!*

Oh hell!

Coiling around the pipe and spiraling upward at one meter per second, the sea-serpent charged from the abyss, emitting a hypnotic spell from its bioluminescent kaleidoscope. The attack would be unavoidable; from this angle, the eel could easily circumnavigate Tad's position, putting itself exactly where it needed to be at any given time to deliver the bone-crunching bite.

Tad was helpless, unable to do anything but stare at

his oncoming demise, entranced by the sinister light show approaching like a freight train.

This is it. This is how I'm going to die.

He was doomed; outsmarted by an accident of nature that should've never existed. As the lights of the sea-serpent soared up from the dark realm, his hands left the pipe. Tad accepted his fate and drifted away from the flowline, waiting calmly for the eel to crush his body and spirit.

Ughhhh!

The world spun around him, the ocean becoming a blur as his suit spiraled out of control. Suddenly, his head jerked unnaturally. Below in the gloom, the glow of the eel had faded. Bubbles surged past his helmet, where he noticed the depth gauge ticking upward at a rapid, impossible rate. Somehow, unbeknownst to Tad, he was now flying at the surface at an inconceivable speed. The eel maintained its pursuit, but his sudden acceleration greatly outmatched his opponent. Within seconds, the strange creature became dulled by the ocean, far out of reach.

When the last lights of the eel died off into the murkiness of the tide, his helmet became flooded with a blinding aura; the under-mounted lights of the rig. Through the visor, he could hear muffled human cries as hands flooded his vision, hauling him from the chaotic waves. With a rough throw, he was hurled over the mesh grating of the rig sub-floor.

Just like that, he was back in the safety of his colleagues, rescued from the turbulent riptide.

"Get his helmet off!" cried Norton, his burly form appearing behind the watery visor. "Come on, Roberts! Tug it like you mean it! Just like you do in your cabin late at night. That's it! Let him breathe!"

With a rush of salty sea air, Tad's helmet was unlatched and yanked from his head. Having cheated death, he stared out in shock at the thirty crew-members, divers, and rig contractors who crowded around him. A few of them had smiles of relief. The others looked like they'd seen a ghost.

"Holy shit, Baron!" Norton laughed at the head of the group. "You better thank the Treadwell management staff for mounting those underwater cameras. We saw that toothy SOB followin' you up! Hawkins here was able to get a winch on your oxygen tank in the nick of time. Hawkins, you earn'd a burger too!"

"Thank you, Sir!" came a grateful cry near the back.

"What... what was that *thing*?" Tad muttered, absorbing what transpired.

"Beats me," Norton admitted, slamming a reassuring hand over on Tad's shoulder. "Some type of electric eel that Treadwell's scientists didn't log. I'd wager its endangered, if not near extinction. Congratulations, Baron. You discovered a new predatory species and lived to tell about it! Damn thing might very well be the apex predator of Okeanos. Now, what's the status of that open valve? Did you seal it?"

"It's not an open valve," Tad answered. "The eel ate away part of the pipeline. Its teeth are very strong."

The crowd erupted in awe, prompting chatter of the dangerous species. A few engineers threw up hands and chuckled, joking their diving careers were over.

"You're tellin' me that thing bit through carbon-steel with those chompers?" Norton asked, running both hands through his balding scalp. "Treadwell's not gonna like this. Any chance you *could*—"

"If you're gonna insist I go back down there with that thing, Mr. Norton, then you're off your rocker," Tad glared. "This goes for *all* of you. No amount of money is worth going down without a naval escort. I wouldn't be surprised if that thing's scales are impervious to spear-guns. Now, if you'll excuse me. I believe there's a cheeseburger, fries, and scotch waiting for me in the mess hall. I might have to take a detour to my quarters first; damn dragon made me shit my pants."

As Tad lumbered out of the sub-floor to the stairwell, he heard Norton's next pep talk begin about how the problem would be resolved—and *who* would be doing the resolving.

Tad cracked a discreet smile.

Unsurprisingly, there were no immediate volunteers.

TRANSFERENCE

BY

JULIAN MICHAEL CARVER

Cute little guy, aren't you?

Naomi looked at the synthetic's head, noting how remarkably close it resembled a department store mannequin. The face was gray with a semi-gloss sheen, reflecting the overhead track lights. Depicted in promo poster artwork, the borosilicate glass eyes would glow with a sapphire hue when activated. The arms—silicone with a titanium skeleton—rested on either side of the chiseled abs. The specimen was impressive; even for an android.

Damn robot puts me to shame, Naomi thought, noting how badly she needed an exercise routine.

"Would you like a brochure?" asked an attractive blonde receptionist. "You must be at least a *little* curious if you wandered in from the mall madness?"

"Sure," Naomi replied, stepping from pedestrian traffic in the hall through the store archway. "What is this place, anyway?"

"Take a seat and I'll tell you about it," the blonde said, gesturing to a stool in front of the receptionist desk.

Naomi sat down, unable to take her eyes from the silicone robot until the blonde handed her a brochure. She thumbed through the pages as the receptionist commenced a sales pitch.

"Our boutique is called *Transference*. It's a new procedure that is fun, simple, and refreshingly unique. Ever wonder what a duplicate version of yourself would be like? Now you can, with a transference procedure. First, you fill out your best traits with our multiple choice two-hundred-word questionnaire. That way we make sure we capture all your dominant attributes up front. Next comes the N.U.P., which stands for Neurological Uplink Phase, but I like to just call it the 'fun part'. It's completely painless. We do it all right here in the back room. There, you are hooked up with nodes to our proprietary memory-link software; an algorithm that scans, traces, and imprints your brain activity to your synthetic double. It captures everything through Magnetic Resonance Imaging and Electroencephalography. An hour later, after your N.U.P. is complete, your synthetic will be ready for use. And that, my dear, is *Transference*."

Naomi smiled. The blonde had rehearsed the speech to perfection.

"I could use a free maid," Naomi chuckled.

"A maid, a friend, whatever you need," the receptionist blushed, biting her lip. "I've even heard testimonials saying how it spiced things up in the bedroom. And before you ask; no—insurance won't cover it."

"How much?"

"It's a little over ten thousand credits," the receptionist admitted. "That includes all necessary application fees and paperwork filing. There's also a five thousand credit cost for the synthetic itself."

"*Youch,*" Naomi winced. "That's a substantial fee."

"It's the twenty-fourth century," the blonde went on. "Household synthetics aren't cheap. Just think of all you could accomplish with two of you walking around. Think of it; your double can remote work while you get housework done. It can run errands for you, get groceries, walk the dog. Synthetics are also built-in security systems. By tapping into your home WiFi, they can alert authorities if a break-in occurs, or EMTs if there's a medical emergency."

"We have a security system," Naomi stated.

"Not like this," she went on. "Let me guess: you have a box on the wall that says 'armed' or 'disarmed' and blares an obnoxious alarm. Sounds fearsome, but not like a synthetic. They'll actually chase away burglars, not just annoy them with sirens."

"Are you a receptionist or a saleswoman?" Naomi laughed.

"Both," the blonde smiled. "It just depends on what my master has me doing."

"Your *master?*"

"Dammit, Sandrine!" yelled a female's voice from the back corridor. "I leave you alone for ten minutes and you're already running more scams!"

A businesswoman stomped into the reception area. Naomi couldn't help but gasp as she came into view.

Both the businesswoman and the receptionist were nearly identical. The only separating characteristics were the hairstyles; the businesswoman was a brunette with short-cropped hair.

"*Uh,* I'm officially freaked out," Naomi admitted, standing from the seat. "You're what, sisters?"

"Hardly," the blonde laughed. "I'm her much better-looking synthetic counterpart."

"You wish," the businesswoman leered, extending a handshake. "I'm Sherri Walters, the entrepreneur behind Transference. This is Sandrine, a prototype for the nextgen synthetics my scientists have cooked up. The nextgens are still in trial phase. When they roll out next year, they'll sweep the nation. Although they'll cost much more due to their customization, they will be in high demand. At least, that's what our market analysts predict in the forecast. I plan to use the nextgens to take Transference public. We're listing on the stock exchange next month. I must apologize for Sandrine. She sweet, but she's also a hustler. The price is twenty-five hundred credits for a Transference procedure. How much did she quote you?"

Naomi looked at Sandrine. The synthetic's eyes portrayed a glimmer of remorse.

A swindling android, she thought. *What will they think of next?*

"She quoted me twenty-five hundred credits," Naomi replied. "And that sounds like a fair price. When can I get started?"

A look of relief washed over Sandrine's artificial face.

"Right now!" Sherri exclaimed. "You're my first customer of the day, and there are no appointments on the books. Follow me to my office and we'll get the boring paperwork over with. And Sandrine, I'm *watching* you! No scheming on the job."

"Yes, master," Sandrine smiled discreetly as Naomi followed Sherri to the back.

Naomi couldn't help but smile when she heard the synthetic greet the next arrival.

"Would you like a brochure?" Sandrine asked the customer. "You must be at least a *little* curious if you wandered in from the mall madness?"

LIGHT WRAP

BY

JULIAN MICHAEL CARVER

The light-tram whisked by on the overpass, aglow against the blue skyline of Zystahl several miles away. Shuffling down the sidewalk, Jack Devlin wobbled forward, hungover and malnourished. A night of alcohol abuse twisted his stomach into knots, while drugs did little to extinguish his splitting headache. He looked like hell, and he knew it.

"Last night of heavy drinking," he said, swearing a promise he knew he couldn't keep. "Just stick with the magic powder, Jack. At least then, you get a longer float-time."

He shuffled past the windows of a rusted-out bus, catching his unkempt appearance. He hadn't managed to shave in the morning. Devlin's afternoon was spent haunting the rim of a toilet bowl. Shaving seemed like an afterthought.

Ahead, the shadows under the overpass illuminated a discreet white van, parked against a wall laden with eroded graffiti. Three men in trench coats awaited around the bullet-ridden van. With matching outfits and hairstyles, Devlin thought they looked more like a cyberpunk-rock band than a fearsome drug cartel. But in reality, the Reaper Syndicate was the deadliest gang in the city's crime-ridden underworld. He had to be cautious if he wanted the goods.

As he lurched down the sidewalk, Devlin noticed a fourth gunman hidden behind the van, staring toward the city spires. As he approached, one of the men said something and pointed, prompting the other three to reach into their trench-coats.

They kept their hands hidden. Devlin guessed they were switching off their safeties.

Four heavy hitters. This shit must be the bomb if they're flexing so much muscle.

He threw his hands up calmly, indicating a peaceful transaction.

Devlin wobbled into a support girder, walking in shadow as the road leveled off. This gave him an adequate view of the four cartel members.

He recognized the central figure as Nikolai Pavlov, leader of the Reaper Syndicate. The large man standing beside Nikolai was his enforcer—Barron Kruger—a large German known for hacking limbs off his adversaries. Devlin caught sight of a hawkbill machete tucked beneath his trench coat, blood hardened on the blade.

Devlin assumed the other two figures were street-level henchmen; hired guns for the evening.

Let's get this over with, Devlin thought, coughing into his elbow. *I hope this doesn't take long...*

"You lost, grifter?" asked a gunman, drawing the handle of an Emancipator-22.

"Sorry to bother you gents," Devlin coughed, stumbling toward them. "I heard you're the only gang in Zystahl who has it."

"Has *what*?" asked Barron, a smirk riding his tattooed jawline. The enforcer looked more like a wrestling champion than a mafioso capo.

"What else?" Devlin fired back, annoyed having to jump through hoops. "The hottest new hallucinogenic to hit the East Side Flats. The star powder everyone's talkin' about. Light Wrap, what else?"

Barron made a move forward. Nikolai blocked him.

"Easy," Nikolai smiled, eyeing Devlin. "Who am I to deny a paying customer? Zeke—the latch."

One of the henchmen nodded, opening the van's slider door. Zeke grabbed a suitcase, moving between Nikolai and Devlin. Nikolai nodded, and Zeke opened the suitcase. Inside was a full compartment of zipped stamp-bags filled with orange crystalline powder.

"The hottest stuff on the Flats," Zeke smiled, "just like you said."

"Light Wrap," Nikolai stated, taking one of the bags in his hand and displaying it proudly. "This shit will keep you high for hours. It'll take you to the stratosphere and back. You'll be coming off it for days. I don't know what festering hole you crawled out of, but make sure you have a warm bed. It's a cold winter. You might be knocked out for a day or so, and you don't wanna freeze to death."

"I know you're ruthless, Mr. Pavlov," Devlin said, studying the bag, "but I didn't hear you were sympathetic."

"What good would I be to my clientele if they weren't crawling back for more?" Nikolai grinned in prideful malevolence. "You're of no use to me dead, grifter. How much do you need?"

"Three bags," Devlin replied, reaching into his pocket.

Barron snapped forward, snatching his arm.

"Easy," Barron grumbled, "I'll get it."

Devlin nodded, trying to ignore the enforcer's nauseating breath. Barron produced several credit slips, counted them, and handed them to Nikolai. The crime-lord gave one back to Devlin.

"Some change," Nikolai smiled. "Be sure to come back and spend it. I have a feeling you will. When you see how far into the galaxy this stuff takes you, you'll be begging for the next fix. Zeke, three bags to this hobo."

Devlin took the bags and shoved them into his coat pocket.

"How long will this last me?"

"Two weeks if you drag it out," the unnamed henchmen piped up. "More like a week and a half for most users with that amount of stamp-bags. We'll be seeing you soon—we guarantee it."

"Something tells me you won't," Devlin muttered, turning to leave.

"Tha' hell's that supposed to mean?" Zeke asked, irritated by the remark.

None of the Reapers noticed Devlin's discreet nod to the bushes across the street. If they had, he'd already be pushing daisies.

In an instant, the vegetation was chopped apart by machine gunfire.

Devlin hit the pavement, burying his head under his elbows. He scrunched into a ball, waiting out the storm. Humming bullets whizzed overhead, hitting concrete walls, the van, and human flesh. A second later, Zeke's bullet-ridden body slammed onto his back, pinning him to the pavement. Devlin cringed, feeling the henchman's torso flopping as the thug bled out.

Through a slit in his fingers, he watched seven shooters appear from the bushes, sending machine gunfire at their targets. He heard one of the Reapers fall, gurgling blood before breaking teeth on the curb.

With the next barrage, the van's windshield exploded into shards, raining glass on his ankles. The two remaining Reapers returned fire. One Reaper was hit immediately, shrieking as he crumpled on the other side of the van. The final shooter exhausted the remainder of his cartridge, dropped his gun, and ran under the overpass. A second later, he was tagged in the shoulder and fell to the concrete.

With the final shooter neutralized, the dark street returned to silence, save for the horn of the distant light-tram.

Devlin felt a tap on his shoulder.

"Targets down, Commander," declared a man clad in tactical attire.

"Good," Devlin replied, standing up and dusting himself off. "Any survivors?"

"Just one."

The team-leader pointed to the van. Several feet away, Barron Kruger was slumped against the bloody passenger door. Several rounds tagged his shoulder, while another punctured his leg. The leg wound was saturated with blood; evidence of a severed femoral artery. His face contorted in a gaunt scowl. As Devlin stood over his wounded competitor, he knew Barron would soon be dead.

The strike team crowded around the final member of the Reaper Syndicate, weapons lowered. Barron made a sluggish move for his discarded Emancipator. A sniper kicked it away, letting the weapon clatter to a storm drain.

"I don't know who you pecker-heads are," Barron spat blood, remaining upright. "But you've got balls. Well, don't pussy out. *Do it!*"

"Do *what?*" Devlin asked. "Put you out of your misery? Not until we know the exact location of your distribution center. Light Wrap will now be manufactured by Dark Blade. You've been relieved of your service, Barron."

"You think I'll talk?" Barron laughed, a gruff cackle of a dying man. "You might be waiting a long time. I'll bleed out before then, Jackass!"

"Sir," said one of the masked gunmen, fishing around near the driver seat. "There's a Coordinate Cube tracker beacon mounted above the flip-down mirror. I guess Nikolai wasn't very trusting of his employees. If the tracking data is any good, it should lead us right to their lab. We'll just see where the van was driven to the most. Odds are, that's their base of operations. I can extract the GPS data back at the rendezvous point."

"Very good, Ken," Devlin smiled, watching fear wash over Barron. "How much firepower you think we'll need?"

"Not much," the team leader replied. "If Nikolai was willing to come out here with just three hitters, I'd wager his operation is small. A few shooters perhaps. The rest will most likely be money counters and lab scientists. We could grab a few more contractors, but honestly, I think we'll be in the clear with the team you've put in place, Jack."

"Excellent," Devlin said, turning to Barron. "Rodney,

one in his head. I hate watching our enemies suffer. It's what sets us apart from other gangs—compassion and swift justice for our enemies. We aren't animals, unlike the butchers from the Reaper Syndicate."

Rodney approached, lifting a pistol to Barron's head. Barron feigned defiance, but as his bowels promptly gave out, Devlin confirmed it was all an act. The man was as unprepared to die as any, and in the end, his bravery was a mask for cowardice. He saw it before, through crime-lords Dark Blade had slaughtered throughout their silent ascension. It had been a bloodbath, spanning months of organized poisonings, car bombings, and ambushes. Finally, with the demise of the Reaper Syndicate, the city was theirs for the taking.

The muzzle flash went off, and Barron's burly corpse tumbled to the road.

"What of the bodies?"another shooter asked.

"Collect them in the van and prepare them for acid," Devlin answered, turning to the city lights. "If we're lucky, Zystahl authorities will assume the action got too hot for the Reapers and they skipped town. Meanwhile, we'll be planning our return. We'll become the most powerful gang this shit-hole has ever seen. Three months, and our product will be in every trap house from here to West End. Our time has come, gentlemen. The return of Dark Blade."

A flurry of clapping rang out under the bridge. Devlin saw that Barron's Emancipator got lodged in the storm drain. He picked it up.

A trophy to remember this momentous occasion.

"Enough celebration for now," he said, sheathing his dead rival's weapon. "We have one more place to hit—their distribution center. Then, the city's ours, boys!"

HOLOCORPS

BY

JULIAN MICHAEL CARVER

Smoke.

More smoke and a flurry of hot tracer rounds.

Smoke and battered artillery equipment.

All directions: Smoke and lingering traces of the prior conflict.

Ground Infantry 5072 thumbed off the safety of his Eradicator pulse rifle, scanning the terrain ahead through the digital scope. Smog loomed on the horizon, amid traces of toppled chemical laser cannons and bombarded fallout shelters.

Amid the remnants of the battle, GI-5072 detected faint traces of movement. Hints of metallic space armor glimmered through the smog cloud, only to scurry down into foxholes or gunnery nests. Enemy reinforcements had arrived and were readying for the next wave of attack. Beyond the enemy trenches, the rumble of a jet-tank engine reverberated over the crackle of flame.

They're coming...

Anticipating jumping back into the fray, he checked

the ammunition counter on the Eradicator's digital screen. Three blasts remaining; hardly enough to take on a regiment of enemy ground troops and inbound tanks. With three detonators left, he was severely unprepared for the enemy's inevitable advance.

GI-5072 sunk down into the foxhole, letting his Eradicator fall harmlessly down the muddy slope. Out of options and wildly outnumbered, he peered off in both directions of the trench. Discarded weaponry and toppled sandbags lay scattered throughout, laden with dirt from mortar fire. The rest of his company had perished in the first battle.

He was alone.

GI-5072 crouched down and weighed his options. He could rummage through the debris and salvage a more adequate weapon to mount a counter-offensive. But that would take time; precious time which was rapidly dwindling. Not to mention, even with the most heroic last stand, he was still *one* man.

One man against an entire contingent of the enemy's best ground troops.

Damn! Time is running out!

Cautiously he cast a glance over the battlefield, witnessing more activity beyond the smog cloud. By now, the first wave of enemy jet-tanks began to waft through the haze. Chrome turrets pierced the smoke a hundred meters away across the basalt flats. Infantry troops were falling into rank-and-file formation as the tank proceeded across the plains.

GI-5072 cussed, slamming a fist down on the dirt.

They're on their way! There isn't enough time to react with strategy. At the rate of jet-tank travel, they'll be on our foxholes in under a minute.

He could run, but running would be cowardly, especially when his CO ordered him to hold the position at all costs. He grabbed his Eradicator and hunkered down in the ditch. Another glance revealed the column had now advanced more than halfway across the expanse. Foot-soldiers began to fan out away from the protection of jet-tanks, emboldened by lack of incoming fire.

GI-5072 gritted his teeth, awaiting the oncoming barrage about to be unleashed upon him. The fight would be fast, he thought, but perhaps a well-placed detonator throw would get lucky and dispatch a tank. Hopeful that his last stand wouldn't be in vain, he pressed the activate button on a detonator, and waited, watching as the counter ticked down to just the right time. Then, winding up, he hurled the chrome ball skyward with all his might, watching as the sphere arced and fell toward the first advancing tank.

"One poor schmuck against my *entire* fifty-second tank regiment?" Potter asked, staring in awe at his foe's debacle. Are you that reckless that you would send that poor soul up against numerous vehicles, not to mention ground support?"

"Hey, if it means bringing your high score down a peg or two," Matty smiled, "then I'm all for it. You've had the HoloCorps high score now for weeks. Quite frankly, I think you need knocked off your high horse."

The two twelve-year-old boys stood in the middle of the spaceport arcade, watching from either end of the illuminated counter. On the tabletop, pixelated figures marched in various directions. Most of them were headed toward Matty, including numerous jet-tanks and a flurry of jogging infantry. On the other side of the table sat Matty's lone soldier, embedded in a shallow trench while frantically lobbing detonators.

Two of the detonators were fortunate enough to destroy the jet-tank at the front of the column. The vehicle glitched and exploded into virtual flames. Under attack, Potter's soldiers halted and crouched, trying to determine where the attack originated.

"You know it's only a matter of time, right?" Potter smiled behind his braces. "Why don't you just surrender now? At least you'll have one soldier going into the next game. You know how expensive buying HoloCorps inventory can be."

"Why do you think you've won so much?" Matty frowned. "You're the only one of our friends with a job, so you can afford to keep buying more holo-packs. The rest of us have to tap into our allowances or birthday cash. Hey, at least I'll go out in a blaze of glory!"

"Very well," Potter smiled. "I'm through toying with you! I've given you enough opportunities to surrender. Now the time has come. All troops, advance!"

"Go for it, GI-5072!" Matty called as holographic activity erupted under the translucent HoloCorps logo. "Give 'em hell!"

WASTE OF LIFE

BY

JULIAN MICHAEL CARVER

Both the human and the AI counterpart were dead.

Vera Tapping stared at the surreal scene in the cold hospital room.

Lying in the bed closest to the wall, Adrian Prescott glared lifelessly at the ceiling. Illuminated by golden lights of a passing hover tram through Venetian blinds, Prescott's death glare concentrated on a water-stained ceiling tile. His skin turned ghostly pale, leading Vera to wonder if rigor mortis had already took hold.

Connected to Prescott via a web of complex cables and clamps was a stagnant six-foot-tall synthetic human shell. Before the ill-fated operation, Vera guessed Prescott procured a sizable fortune. Synthetic human shells were costly. The model was a newer DigiSync brand AI-5, released for the general market two months prior. DigiSync AI's were the most popular brand for memory sharing by far. Vera recalled the AI-4 earning high praise during its three year run.

Had the MTP—Memory Transfer Protocol—gone as

planned, the AI-5 shell would have been fully operational. Adrian's memory, personality, and theoretically, soul, would be transferred to the robot.

Vera frowned, making a note with a holopen on her digital tablet. She wrote that yet another fatality occurred with the newest innovation in artificial implant technology: Optimal Memory and Body Sharing—the process of transferring your memories, thoughts, and intellect—into the body of a bipedal robot. Problems with this new procedure had been rampant regardless of the manufacturer.

Another case of techies rushing approval stages and skipping trial testing before green-lighting it, Vera thought, inspecting the scene. *There should be more strict bylaws and regulations on these transfer operations.*

Since the Technological Renaissance of the late 2200s, procedures involving tech infusing with humans had grown popular in North America. Now, in 2301, the idea of living forever as a robotic intelligence piqued the world's interest. Ninety-five percent of the time, the procedures were completed without fail.

The unlucky man, Adrian Prescott, was an up-and-coming entrepreneur; a nightclub owner in the budding Cultural District. Before his demise, Adrian informed the hospital staff and on-call doctor that he had been financing for the operation for years. He accomplished this through a mix of dividend passive income and growth stocks. Vera had been genuinely impressed by this feat of financial management. Up until now, she assumed only CEOs for multinational conglomerates were able to afford the procedure.

Her thoughts were interrupted by the intense mastication of her partner, Detective Ricardo Scott. Ricardo, or "Ricky" as she called him, had recently given up smoking in favor of bubble gum. Smacking a large wad in his mouth, Ricky continued his questioning. In front of him sat Suzanne Cornell, general manager of Oakhill hospital and a nurse whose brass name-tag read 'Juanita - RN'.

"You sure no one had access to him?" Ricky asked, munching obnoxiously. "As a nightclub owner, I've been told Mr. Prescott had his share of enemies. Everyone from the mob to jealous husbands wanted their shot at this bloke."

"No one else had access," insisted Suzanne. "After Juanita secured Mr. Prescott to the transfer monitor with the AI, our software gave her the green light to initialize the MTP. The transfer was completed without hiccup, as you can see by the dialog box on the monitor. Completely full and green, indicating the patient's transfer was successful."

Suzanne pointed to the outdated terminal beside the bed containing the lifeless synthetic shell. Vera leaned in, inspecting the dialog box. The panel contained a completed transfer progress bar. Below the bar, the computer displayed a coded message.

MTP complete. Recovery Process beginning now.

"I'm guessing this isn't what an ideal recovery process looks like?" Vera asked, pointing to Adrian's catatonic body.

Suzanne shot her a cold, deliberate glare.

"I hope you can appreciate the transparency on our part. We've been very open as far as I'm aware. I can assure you there is no negligence on our part. This instance was a fluke."

"That has yet to be determined," Ricky replied, making another note with his holopen. "How's your cyber security?"

"Pardon?"

"Your cyber-security unit," Ricky added. "A common problem with MTP sessions we've found are intrusive viruses that intercept data mid-transfer. They are often the root of the core problem. Death can be a common outcome."

Judging by the outdated diamond wallpaper and twenty-year-old lagging software, Vera judged that a cyber security team wasn't in Suzanne's arsenal.

"*Uh*, well there is *a—*"

"Suzanne, Juanita," Vera interrupted. "Thank you for your help. Can you give my partner and I the room? We have forensic analysts and photographers en route. After they're gone, we'll reconvene, just to go over some things. There may be a need for more statements to be logged. In the meantime, thank you for your cooperation in this unraveling case."

"Oh, okay," Suzanne replied with a look of relief. "Let's go, Juanita. Thank you, detectives."

"Why did you do that?" Ricky asked after they left the two detectives. "Why do I ask? You have another one of your hunches, don't you, Tapping?"

"You know me too well," Vera smiled.

She walked over to the computer terminal and sat down on the worn chair. Typing commands, she navigated through the MTP interface.

"We really should wait for forensics," Ricky suggested. "What are you up to?"

"I already downloaded the data files to my tablet," Vera replied, waving off any fear of crime scene contamination. "We will have the exact computer settings for later analysis. If there's something amiss, we'll catch it."

"How can you be sure you didn't screw something up?"

"My undergrad was data administration, Ricky," Vera smiled. "I know these servers well. Trust me, I have an *exact* digital footprint of their setup saved to my database."

"I take it you don't think it's a cyber security issue?" Ricky asked, popping gum while leaning over her shoulder.

"Likely not," replied Vera, scrolling through the folder hierarchy for abnormalities. "If you read the initial briefings on MTP fatalities—which I'm sure you didn't—you'd remember when viruses are present, completion failure will be the outcome. Yet here, the status bar completed as scheduled. Something isn't adding up."

"What about a wiring failure?" Ricky suggested. "Those cables look pretty sloppy. Are they all plugged in correctly?"

"Again," Vera said, "if that were true, the completion bar wouldn't have finished the task. Hell, it wouldn't have even started."

"Dammit," Ricky cursed. "Maybe Suzanne is right.

Maybe it was just a fluke. Who knows with these old computers? Maybe a spark plug blew a gasket in the server tower. Faulty drive."

"It's a computer, Ricky, not a grav-mower," Vera chuckled, standing up and walking beside the cadaver. "No, this is something else. Some wild card we've not encountered with these troublesome protocols. I'm gonna have another look at the bed. There must be something we're missing."

"Forensics will be here soon," Ricky assured her, jotting more notes. "Maybe one of those young hotshots will have some insight. Go ahead and poke around. Maybe you'll get lucky. And are you sure that computers *don't* have spark plugs?"

Vera ignored her partner's attempt at lightening the mood.

She leaned over the bed, inspecting Adrian's corpse for negligence or foul play. Hologram readings on the bedside terminal indicated zero signs of life. Vera decided this was probably normal, since the businessman's intellect should be transferred to the AI. But the DigiSync panel wasn't reading life signs either, indicating an empty server with zero memory files.

A completed transfer, yet zero signs of life for both Adrian Prescott and his AI counterpart. What the hell is going on here?

Vera turned to the wiring connectors, deciding maybe Ricky was onto something with his spark plug comment. She perused the power couplings and data cables. The cables were properly secured and suction-cupped to the pale forehead of the corpse.

"What the hell happened here?" Vera mumbled.

Ricky ignored her, sitting down at the outdated terminal to reevaluate the process setup.

What could've happened? Vera thought, narrowing her eyes on the power connection. *Could it be something small and easily overlooked? Maybe it was a mob hit. He could've been poisoned the day before, but the actual death took place now—during the MTP process. Mafia activity has escalated in recent years. It's possible. Maybe forensics will find evidence of—*

"Anything?" Ricky asked, walking over as she knelt beside the bed frame.

"Nothing that pops up as obvious, I'm afraid," Vera replied. "I hate waiting for forensics and CSI, Ricky! I love solving these medical cases on the spot before the cavalry arrives. It gives me a sense of fulfillment, you know?"

"Oh, I know," Ricky laughed, "because I'm the same way! That's why we make good partners! Say, where's the waste receptacle? This gums lost its taste."

"Should be one over by the door."

"There wasn't," Ricky replied, looking around. "Oh, good. Here's one behind the bed. The little thing got tipped over."

Vera saw that Ricky was correct. Behind the hospital bed was a toppled Mk. T-17 trash and recycling receptacle robot. Its contents partially spilled over the tile, the tiny machine had been knocked over somehow behind the bed.

The robot beeped its speakers softly in automated distress. Vera put the loose trash back into the lid, before picking up the foot-tall cylinder and set it upright. She held the lid ajar as Ricky spat his chewing gum, before the machine's top closed automatically.

As the opening closed, an odd warning flashed on its readout screen. Vera squinted, trying to make sense of it.

It was a flurry of blinking exclamation points, numbers, and letters that scrolled across. Below the random characters in a smaller font size, an error code presented itself: *ERR 21—memory bank full.*

"Memory bank full," Vera said. "Trash receptacles typically don't have inserted memory. All they have is basic code for movement and for scanning surroundings. *Whoa!* Ricky, pull that transfer dialogue box back up! I'll call Suzanne and Juanita back in here! I think I just cracked this case wide open!"

She raced over to the door and pulled it open, waving Suzanne and Juanita back into the room. By the time they arrived, Ricky pulled up the terminal information.

"Okay, Vera," he said, operating the hover-mouse. "What am I doing here? Direct me."

"Pull up the transfer settings," Vera pointed with the trash receptacle tucked under her arm. "Should be minimized under the completion bar. There, good! Open the protocol tab. Good."

"What's the thought here, Detective?" Suzanne asked. "You think our programs are 'trash'?"

Juanita tried not to laugh, biting her lip.

"Not your *programs*," Vera replied, "just your patient. Thanks, Ricky. Okay, let me see here. *Aha!* Bingo. Wireless!"

"*Wireless?*"

"Yes, Mrs. Corbell. Whoever set up this program had it set for a wireless override by default, instead of choosing the wired connection. The wired connection is *always* preferred by manufacturers. In the case of Adrian Prescott, this proved problematic. You're running outdated software here; programs that can't detect the numerous smart robotics you have running amok here in the suites. That's what happened with this T-17 receptacle robot. The T-17 must have stumbled inside just as Adrian's MTP transfer initiated. Since I'm guessing your computers haven't been updated in some time, the T-17's wireless transmitter tapped into the MTP, overriding the entire process. This explains why Adrian's body and the DigiSync AI-5 are showing zero signs of life."

"Am I missing something?" Suzanne asked, dumbfounded by the realization.

"Mrs. Corbell," Vera said calmly, holding up the T-17 so she could see the receptacle's screen. "You're staff transferred Adrian into this receptacle's computer."

She pressed a button on the T-17's panel, resetting the message. Suzanne's eyes lit up as the panel displayed a new line of text.

"Help me! I'm in the damn trash can! Can you say, lawsuit?"

Good job, Tapping!" Ricky applauded her. "You solved the case after all!"

"Oh *no!*" Suzanne cried, fingers fanning through her white hair. " Juanita, you should've checked the damn settings!"

Juanita looked bewildered and terrified. She opened her mouth, but couldn't form words to convey her shock.

"Detective," Suzanne went on, "Please tell me—can you complete the transfer to the correct AI? Oh, I feel horrible! I hope he didn't suffer!"

"The only suffering he did was when someone kicked over the trash can," Vera laughed. "Rigor mortis appears to have set into his human body, so unfortunately, he can't reverse the procedure. I can get him to the AI's body, but I'll have to take him to the Cyber Division in Uptown. There they have up-to-date equipment and software that can correctly process these transfers. In other words, Mrs. Corbell, if you want to include MTP transfers as hospital services, you better make sure the *correct* processes are selected. Otherwise, your intrusive custodial robotics will find the incompatibilities, exposing your shortcomings."

"Not to mention leaving you wide open for liability," Ricky added.

With her stern warning, Vera followed Ricky out the door, carrying the receptacle robot known as Adrian Prescott tucked under her arm.

TYRANT LIZARD

BY

JULIAN MICHAEL CARVER

Nothing in the field manual could've prepared me for this!

The roar of the tyrannosaur was breathtaking; a testament to the carnivore's dominant prowess in the vast wilderness of the Late Cretaceous.

Alexis Hasapis—who was standing in a wide-open field—dropped her video recorder in fright, letting it vanish under the veil of dennstaedtiaceous ferns. Around her, the hadrosaur herd she had been documenting began to fidget and moan. A few juvenile hadrosaurs wailed in protest, while their parents nudged them with their bills, aware of the danger lurking beyond the thicket. The herd, numbering over thirty hadrosaurs, began to stray from the jungle barrier. In fright, they trampled up the slope toward the summit of the hill, directly toward the perimeter fence of the base camp.

Stay with the tyrannosaur, Lex. You have enough hadrosaur footage to fill a twenty-terra hard-drive. But hell, if that roar didn't sound close!

She tried to regulate her breathing, but that was easier said than done. They heard tyrannosaur calls for the past week, but none in such close vicinity to the encampment as the roar she just heard. Four days earlier, Will Ross claimed to have spotted a rex through binocular-vision passing by the adjacent valley. Alexis didn't put much stock in the claims. Ross was known to exaggerate to build excitement and gain clout. This time around, she was certain everyone on the hill heard it. And with the entire contingent of workers concentrated at the base camp, she would be alone to experience the colossal predator without the safety of the perimeter fence.

I bet that old thing couldn't even hold back the hadrosaurs, she thought. *Let alone a fully mature tyrannosaur that could just leap-frog right over it. They really should've given us more defensive tools as opposed to these dinky cattle-prods.*

A second later, another rumble belched from the forest's edge. The growl—which Alexis likened to a freight locomotive blaring through a bull-horn—was undoubtedly the most horrific sound she'd ever heard. It was loud, tough, and clearly originated from a confident carnivore in its prime.

Where are you? Where are you?

As Alexis debated running for safety, she dove for her recorder. After ten seconds of searching, she finally located the camera's muddy neck-strap under the fern fronds, keeping her gaze locked on the sycamore trees. As the last adult hadrosaur galloped by, she caught a glimpse of a large shadow sauntering under the branches. Discreetly placing the camera strap over her head and around her neck, Alexis trembled backward.

If only Caruthers could see me now! He'd never be down in the glade with an adult t.rex on the loose!

From what she could discern through the thicket, the tyrannosaur reached an impressive height, disturbing branches at least twelve feet above with its gargantuan snout. Even seventy yards into the dense forest, the carnivore's thunderous steps sent shock-waves rippling in its wake. The carnivore's footsteps prompted more wails from the retreating herd.

Alexis resolved not to back up any further. She knew Caruthers and the lead scientists would reprimand her for this, but then she imagined them reviewing her footage, congratulating her for video-documenting a fully-grown tyrannosaurus. Her footage would be the first clip captured of the famed predator since the expedition commenced—or ever, for that matter. She could smell awards, and certainly a hefty pay raise.

Get a shot of the bloody thing, Lex, she mused, quivering as she reached for the record button. *It won't see you if you won't move. That's a thing, right? Oh hell, just get ten seconds of video, then head back to the base camp before the big lug gets too close!*

She brought the camera to bear, flipping open the viewfinder and confirming the large shadow nestled in the safe-zones at center frame. She manipulated the focus ring, confirming the immense carnivore was crystal clear when the digital marching ants effect surrounded the animal's silhouette. When the red *RECORD* button flashed in the upper right, Alexis confirmed the momentous event was being documented.

Battery life good. Thirty minutes of recording time left. 10K resolution. Everything looks good so far.

She debated scrolling through the shots of the hadrosaurs on the viewfinder and deleting everything from that day. She had six days worth of hadrosaur footage, and the herd hadn't done anything particularly noteworthy that day to warrant keeping the massive files, but she ultimately decided against it. The tyrannosaur could vanish at any time, making every second of rolling video valuable for paleo-research. Not to mention, any captured footage of the carnivore would immediately distinguish her as the most valuable member on the expedition, ensuring her return for the next TimeGate shift-change.

Three separate teams had been deployed simultaneously to the Late Cretaceous from TimeSync Industries; a paleontology wing, a technological and engineering division, and, of course, a photography and film-making crew. Alexis was selected last minute as a junior videographer, a contract role that commanded a deluge of background checks with a monsoon of paperwork. She accepted the position less than forty-eight hours before the operation began. The primary objective of the expedition was to document the findings, extract dung, and collect traces of extinct or unclassified flora. All this had to be done while staying in close proximity to the TimeGate and base camp located atop the hill.

And hey, here's a few dinky cattle-prods to stave off the big chompy-chomps, Alexis recalled thinking the day she passed through the time-loop.

The TimeGate was, quite arguably, the most impressive modern marvel developed by TimeSync Industries; a company dedicated to understanding ancient ecology to preserve Earth's present day climate. Built within a twelve-meter-tall steel ring, the TimeGate enabled time-travel by means of a wormhole-generated propulsion system, rendering objects, both living and inanimate, into bits of trans-coded data. The data was then processed and teleported to a specific spacial era in time dictated by user input at the speed of light. Once the TimeGate successfully deployed a wormhole to the Late Cretaceous, parts of a second TimeGate were shipped through, along with a construction crew with a security detail. After the second TimeGate was erected, back-and-forth travel was now possible, but only to that exact point in prehistory.

When Alexis first heard of the remarkable innovation, she was informed the technology was conceived through experimentation with quantum physics and simultaneity mathematics. A conspiracy theorist herself, she found it vague and unlikely, citing nothing short of reverse-engineered alien technology.

After being debriefed on the dangers of the Cretaceous, she met the fifty-seven members with whom she would be camping, including the ten contractors of the documentary crew. Most she clicked with. Some she didn't, including the bombastic, brash lead scientist; Tom Caruthers, whom

TimeSync tasked with heading up the risky operation. But to be fair, most people on the operation didn't get along with Caruthers; they only tolerated him, or rather, lived among him, enduring his pretentious day-to-day demands.

One such demand was dispatching Alexis to the base of the hill to document the herd. Alexis was initially resistant, seeing it as a chore. The herd had been loitering around the field for days. Of course, when the hadrosaurs were first spotted, everyone was overjoyed. But when the herd became the only prehistoric animal sighting—apart from the occasional distant pterosaur—to be seen by the personnel, the excitement soon wore off. She had plenty of hadrosaur footage to appease the suits back at TimeSync. After hearing the roar of the tyrannosaur, she took it as a sign that she was meant to be at the field at that *exact* moment. Had she been back on the plateau at the time of the carnivore's approach, Caruthers would've never authorized her departure to the sycamores. She was a risk-taker, and By-The-Books Caruthers hated that about her.

Now as she stood in the presence of a fully-grown tyrannosaur, Alexis wondered. Had she finally gone too far?

It's not too late to turn back. No! Just shut up and keep rolling!

Slowly the hulking behemoth came into view amid the shadows of conifer branches. Alexis felt her knees quivering, instinctively taking a step back. Now forty yards into the forest and pausing to survey the savanna, she beheld the beast's true appearance.

The tyrannosaur stood at an impressive twenty feet in height, towering over the bramble patches of ferns and ginkgoes. An array of green and brown scales lined its muscular frame, culminating to a large saw-back pattern that jutted along its dorsal vertebrae. Even with a closed jaw, her camera focused in around the ring of razor-sharp teeth, some tinted with a coating of fresh blood. Surprisingly, she found the creature had no feathers—a theory quite controversial and hotly contested in recent decades. She found a second attribute puzzling; atop its snout sat a small golden crest; something Alexis was unfamiliar with regarding tyrannosaur anatomy.

A distant relative of t.rex perhaps? she thought. Is this an undiscovered species? Another link in the cladogram yet to be identified!

With an arrogant swagger, the tyrannosaur lumbered closer, moving meters ahead with ease, snout wobbling up and down as it proceeded toward the treeline. Through shards of light that filtered through the canopy, Alexis became entranced by the sight of its bone-crunching maw, capable of delivering an estimated bite-force of over thirty thousand newtons. It took a little more than a few seconds for the carnivore to cut the distance by half, its thunderous footfalls creating heavy aftershocks.

Behind her, she could hear the hadrosaurs beginning to whine.

Cursing at her cowardice, Alexis noticed she had started backing up again, unable to combat the primal fear tightening her abdomen.

Stay still, dammit! It might pass by! This is the money shot!

Suddenly it hit her—the TimeSync base camp on the hill's plateau was about to become the focal point of the incident. The hadrosaur herd headed uphill, toward the small encampment of fifteen field tents all nestled beside a mobile RV command center and the TimeGate. If the tyrannosaur passed her by and headed up the hillside after the herd, it would come in direct contact with the encampment. With modern time-jump technology currently running protocols with a wait-time of an hour between each charge, the research team would only have enough juice for one portal activation before the carnivore arrived. The team would be forced to wait for her, potentially having to face the tyrannosaur with only a handful of high-voltage staffs.

A few glorified cattle prods to fight off a t.rex? My God! I'm putting the whole team at risk!

In a panic, she spun around.

At the top of the knoll, she saw a pair of frantic

hands waving to her through the tall foliage. It was her photographer and colleague, Manuel Friedman, motioning like a lunatic for her to hurry. The hadrosaur herd was quickly climbing the slope, converging toward the base camp. A flurry of human activity was transpiring behind the tents. Protective cases were being crammed with research material. Devices were being dismantled. A man with terrible posture—Caruthers—was en route to the TimeGate initialization module, preparing the iris for launch. An impromptu departure was about to occur, quite possibly without her!

Do they know the Rex is about to come through? They heard a roar, sure, but why the sudden evac'? Unless—

Another reptilian roar reverberated through the valley, sending Arambourgiana pterosaurs springing from tree-tops. The second cry didn't originate from the tyrannosaur she had been documenting, but from somewhere else. It sounded parallel to her position in the savanna, on the adjacent end of the TimeSync encampment. Her jaw dropped at the horrible timing and of the disaster that was about to unfold. Worst of all: she was alarmingly far from the TimeGate.

There's a second rex coming up the other end of the slope! It's an ambush!

Before she could fully comprehend the danger of her actions, Alexis bolted up the hillside, tearing recklessly through fern fronds. She saw Manuel manage a smile, knowing that his colleague comprehended the danger, before darting for his tent.

Alexis doubled her sprint, fearing the tyrannosaur would be instigated by her acceleration.

In seconds, she reached the first of the hadrosaurs.

Then she heard it. From the forest's edge at the base of the prairie, the first tyrannosaur took notice of her movement and the hadrosaur herd. Instantly the dreaded earth-shaking footfalls started. Branches splintered apart by the predator's flight. Alexis grimaced, likening the cacophony to a subterranean rift from an earthquake.

Please no!

She tore past the first hadrosaurs, clumsily tripping over the brown tail of a juvenile. The herbivores remained still for a second—until the rex crashed through the opening like a wrecking ball to a bricked dwelling.

Wailing in fright, the dinosaurs on the outskirts began galloping up the hill, starting with a slow jaunt before increasing to a frenetic stampede. The entire hillside became a blur of commotion as Alexis became enveloped in the herd's clustered center. Their destination: the TimeSync base camp directly ahead.

The tyrannosaur wasted no time announcing its intentions, belching another hunting cry across the prairie. The carnivore was running at a full-on sprint, pounding the slope as its guttural rumbling grew louder, goaded by its herd's retreat. Alexis quickened her sprint, knowing if she tripped the stampede would crush her. And with hadrosaurs weighing over fifteen thousand pounds each, her death would be quick.

Twenty yards from Manuel's tent, Alexis looked back again.

The rex was absolutely breathtaking, a perfect harbinger of power and destruction. Launching up the slope with a terrifying speed amid well-placed strides, the carnivore's bold approach made the juveniles squeal. Still, even though the animal brought death, Alexis was astounded at its beauty. Sunlight glinted off its radiant green coat, twinkling off the saw-back plates as if it were coated with flawless emeralds. Its maw bumbled up and down like yaw to a Cessna, and its tail swayed with perfect symmetry and deadly elegance.

Turning away, she gritted her teeth, flailing wildly through the tall ferns. With such broad strides, the carnivore would reach her position in no time.

As Alexis reached the front of the stampede, the perimeter fence flew at her in a flash. With a running leap, she dove over the four-foot-high barrier, recovering with a clumsy side-roll before resuming her flight. Then, as she predicted, the fence exploded under pressure. Rammed by the herd, hadrosaur after hadrosaur besieged the barrier, sending high carbon steel cable flinging in all directions. Some hadrosaurs were whipped by the loose cable, yelping in pain as if a lion-tamer cracked them. Others held a healthy fear of the tyrannosaur, forcing their way into the opening—commencing a fresh stampede directly into the TimeSync base camp.

"*Auugh!*"

Yowling as her foot struck a stone, Alexis went airborne, tumbling into the clearing. Eating dirt, she was promptly yanked up by a pair of hands. It was Manuel Friedman, sweat-laden and under siege from a mosquito cloud.

By either fate or divine intervention, the hadrosaurs parted around her, proceeding into the encampment and prompting screams from TimeSync personnel.

"'Bout time, Lex!" Manuel screeched, his safari outfit soaked with perspiration.

"Sorry! I didn't know there was a second rex!" Alexis shrieked, as the herd surged by her shoulders on both sides, stampeding through tents and toppling satellite tripod stands.

As if on queue, the mobile command center ahead received a powerful unseen impact. Inside, Alexis saw the driver of the RV—a former Phoenix bus driver named Denny Richards—scream as he was thrown from his seat, buried with a shower of paperwork stashed above the mirror. Without warning, the vehicle began to tip over, just as two scientists ran out the side door. The vehicle's wheels groaned and creaked, forced over from a hidden folcrum with immense strength. Both scientists dove away from the trailer's edge, just as the command center slammed on its siderevealing the second adult tyrannosaur.

"You were right, Lex," Manuel gulped, mosquitoes plaguing his brow. "We needed more protection before we embarked on this *suicide* operation."

The creature, mirroring the appearance of the first tyrannosaur, uttered a loud roar, relishing in the vehicle's destruction. The entire base camp had become a cauldron of danger, as TimeSync personnel found themselves in a battle ground of rambunctious herbivores and two apex predators.

"*Heads up!*" cried the gruff voice of Tom Caruthers through a megaphone.

Alexis looked to her right, spying her annoying boss atop the control module beside the TimeGate. His hair was disheveled, and his departure bag was already packed and slung over his shoulder.

"Time-jump initialization activating!" he screamed through the megaphone. "We can't risk any of these animals getting back to the present, but we *can't* stay here! I'm setting the decay settings for two minutes, people! Get through the wormhole by then or you're toast! Time-sync discovered. Link has been cleared by TimeSync HQ for immediate evac. Initializing wormhole now. Stand clear."

WHOOOOOOSH!

Just beside the console platform, the TimeGate rim came to life. With a wave of translucent molecular particles bathed in a white haze, each emitter relayed data to the center of the rim, creating a mesmerizing vortex; a rift in time spawning a single route of travel. Rippling to life, the white puddle created an outer glow around the core; a glowing orb where the users could pass through. To Alexis, it looked like a door to the afterlife—the only chance to escape the primeval nightmare.

Above, a green light blinked on, indicating a time-loop had been properly synced with the opposite TimeGate. A route of travel had been determined, linked to a TimeSync Industries warehouse outside of present day Phoenix, Arizona.

"Tom, *watch out!*"

"Everyone!" Caruthers bellowed, raising the megaphone. "Head for the *porta*—"

Caruthers spat blood as entire body was hoisted effortlessly from the platform, snatched up in the maw of the first tyrannosaur, only steps from the TimeGate. The speed at which the massive carnivore plucked the flailing man from the air was astounding; like a pelican gulping up a minnow. Caruthers only managed a helpless incomprehensible murmur as the beast's jaws crunched down, crushing his rib cage while sending a goop of blood drizzling over the control console. After thrashing Caruthers' corpse like a dog with a chew toy, the tyrannosaur stepped off the platform, coming dangerously close to the portal eye. In doing so, the beast's tail flailed, smacking off the TimeGate rim. Sparks erupted from exhaust ports and circuity, threatening to disrupt the time-sync. The wormhole held, but flickered with uncertainty.

"Damn beastie might screw up the time-sync!" Manuel cried.

A pair of research assistants, Ray and Lisa, were the first to try their luck at escape. The pair cautiously approached from the side, lugging along backpacks full of equipment and valuable specimen canisters. The first tyrannosaur turned away, distracted by a hadrosaur lodged in a tent. Ray and Lisa seized the opportunity, running for the active time-loop.

Lisa made it safely, vanishing through the aura shortly thereafter.

Ray wasn't so fortunate.

"Auuugh!"

As the tyrannosaur turned, its tail whipped around like a heavy steel girder tethered to a crane's trolley. Lisa saw the calamity coming and managed to duck. Ray failed to see the danger, receiving the brunt of the creature's involuntary spasm squarely in the chest. An airless gasp escaping his lungs, Ray was flung carelessly across the base camp, airborne at an altitude of twenty feet. Like a comet, his body soared across the sky until vanishing over a disheveled tent, landing somewhere along the southern-facing slope. Alexis gasped, knowing he'd be dead on impact, if not earlier.

The entire base camp—which had been in impeccable shape a minute earlier—had become a battered collage of ramshackle dwellings, toppled tables, and faulty transmission equipment. Hadrosaurs weaved through the ruins while wailing as they slunk by the tyrannosaurs, trying to pinpoint a safe course to the prairie. A few technicians successfully avoided the pair of rexes, arriving at the TimeGate before dematerializing into the haze. A handful of others were limping to the wormhole stairwell, wounded from the stampede.

The first tyrannosaur successfully cornered the hadrosaur trapped in the tent, biting down blindly on the tarp. The tent convulsed before coming to rest, permitting the carnivore to eviscerate the dwelling to maul the creature within.

The second tyrannosaur stepped onto the toppled mobile command center, indenting the siding inward while shattering the glass windows with its mighty foot. Chomping wildly, Alexis saw its jaws clamp down on a fleeing hadrosaur tail. The animal yelped in fear as the carnivore pounced, just as Manuel yanked her away from his tent toward the TimeGate.

"Now's our chance!" he cried, "before the portal decay rate starts! It's already been thirty seconds!"

Alexis turned to flee, but not before spying a helpless victim of the second tyrannosaur's invasion—Denny Richards—still trapped inside the downed RV. Behind the cracked windshield, he screamed helplessly. Denny's bloody face went pale as he saw the caged pendant light above the TimeGate transition from green to yellow. The portal decay rate would soon commence. Denny, an older contracted worker who was now both wounded and entrapped, would never make it. Since the mobile command center had flipped, one side hatch was now inaccessible, facing the ground. The second was facing the sky, and she doubted he'd be able to climb in his wounded state. She was unsure why he couldn't climb out the driver's side door, but there would be time to ask him later over drinks in Phoenix if they survived.

"Denny's still trapped inside!" Alexis cried, pointing to the opposite edge of the camp where the command center remained stagnant.

"Are you blind?" Manuel screeched. "He's a *goner!* And so are we if we don't evacuate!"

"You go then!" Alexis cried, shoving him toward

to TimeGate stairwell. "I'm partly responsible for the delayed evacuation. Everyone stayed behind waiting for *me*, Manuel, including Denny! I can't abandon him here to die."

Manuel started to protest, but Alexis had already cut him off, treading across the trampled clearing. The second tyrannosaur's tail swung across as the carnivore crunched down on the flank of the unfortunate hadrosaur. Alexis ducked, avoiding Ray's fate as the mighty trunk flung a foot above her head. She blinked at the gust, feeling her ponytail thrashing in the windy aftermath. She let it pass overhead before standing erect, resuming her sprint. Like a track and field athlete, she leaped from the ground, clasping the roof's edge with both hands.

"*Ugggh!*"

Gravity sucked her down, until she was propped up from a sudden force from below. Rolling onto the roof—formerly the side—of the RV, Alexis looked down. Manuel was standing below, hoisting his out-of-shape body as best he could up the aluminum siding.

"You came back!"

"Don't wait for me!" he cried, heaving his way up. "Get him out!"

As Manuel kicked his way up, Alexis turned toward the sky-facing side door. Inside, she could hear Denny's muffled screams. She wasted no grabbing the entry handle and flinging open the door. Eight feet below stood a shadowy man, obviously injured.

"Alexis! Am I glad to see your pretty smile."

"Save the flattery, D'!" Alexis laughed, hoisting her body into the opening before free-falling into the void.

With a bang, she landed on the riveted floor beside Denny. In the dim lighting, she could see the left side of his face was a mess of glass shards embedded between wrinkle seams. He had a limp when he walked, undoubtedly from when the tyrannosaur head-butted the RV and sent him flipping over.

The inside of the vehicle had become a disorganized heap of debris. Paperwork, shattered vials, laboratory equipment, and food rations were flung everywhere within the dark command center, illuminated by a single flickering desk lamp with a tungsten bulb. Through the spiderweb cracks in the windshield, Alexis saw the yellow light of the TimeGate had begun flickering. She gritted her teeth, understanding the time-crunch she just assigned herself. The portal wouldn't be active for long.

"There isn't a way out through the front?" Alexis asked her limping colleague.

"No," Denny shook his head. "Rex royally screwed up the driver-side door and it won't open. Other door is buried in the ground. Front pane is made up of reinforced polycarbonate bulletproof glass. It'll spider-web, but it's shatterproof. Only way out is through the side hatch you just came through."

He pointed up. To her relief, Manuel was standing six feet above them with an extended hand.

"What are you waiting for?" he cried, sweat drenching his safari clothes. "Take *my*—"

"*Manuel!*"

In a splash of blood Manuel was gone, swept up in the shadowy jaws of the tyrannosaur. In the blink of an eye, both the scientist and the dinosaur's colossal head vanished from the hatch. Alexis grimaced, aghast as a droplet of her colleague's blood pricked her cheek.

Manuel's screams became muffled as the carnivore carried him away from the command center, coming to an abrupt end five seconds after. Alexis stared in disbelief through the open hatch to the sky.

"He's *gone*," she uttered, lips trembling. "Manuel is— *ouch!*"

A sharp pain hit Alexis in her knee, jolting her from the stupor.

"Sorry," Denny apologized, lugging out a table from the corner. "I just realized these tables can come off the wall by these release latches. We can mourn Manuel on the other side of the TimeGate, Lexi, but that time isn't now. Help an old man up, will you?"

She nodded, fighting off the shock of Manuel's death.

Denny was right. Her friend was dead, but if they didn't haul ass to the TimeGate, she might experience the same fate.

Alexis helped the wounded man step from an office chair to the tabletop. He steadied his footing by means of wall support, just as she hopped up after him. The table held strong, supporting both their weight as they surveyed the next problem—hobbling through the skylight without becoming a *t.rex* snack. Offering a hand for his feet, Alexis braced herself as Denny's boot pressed into her palms. Despite the limp, the older man was somewhat nimble, spring-boarding from her hand to the hatch.

After whirling around, he fired a hand back down, helping her through. With a hard tug, Denny hauled her through the hatch. On the rooftop above, she beheld a terrible sight.

"*Awh'* hell," Denny muttered, skin turning white as he stood upright.

The campsite had become a bloodbath of twisted corpses, both human and hadrosaur. Arms, legs, and limbs lay scattered throughout the trodden campsite, laden with shredded fragments from tarp tents and discarded equipment. The area was completely devoid of human activity. The remainder of the TimeSync expedition had either evacuated through the TimeGate or had been slain while attempting to flee.

At the foot of the TimeGate stairs, both tyrannosaurs were engaged in a fierce competition of tug-of-war—with the rope being the hardly recognizable corpse of Manuel. With the splintering sound of bone, the dead man broke asunder, sending ligaments, entrails, and organs slathering over the field.

"How are we gonna get you *dow*—"

Without announcing his plan, Denny willingly took the plunge. Alexis cringed as he rocketed to the soil below, directly beside the exposed rib cage of a mauled hadrosaur. After his crash-landing, the old man rolled with a theatrical somersault. After competing the roll, he used the carcass to prop himself back up, miraculously avoiding further injury.

Alexis found the maneuver remarkable, worried that she wouldn't be able to accomplish the same feat.

Suddenly, a warning klaxon blared at the TimeGate. The yellow light flickered to an ominous red, casting a crimson sheen over the rim of the portal eye. The white vortex began to flicker, sending wisps of icy lightning sparking from conductors.

Alexis grimaced, realizing the portal decay rate had begun. They had less than forty seconds to enter the time-loop before the wormhole disengaged. An hour would have to lapse before the TimeGate could be restarted.

Hell. I don't know if I'll be alive that long!

"What are you waitin' for, kid?" Denny's voice broke through the chaos. "*Jump!*"

Alexis held her breath as she leaped from the RV's upper lip, bracing herself as the ground rushed forward.

"*Oo-f!*"

Her shoulder, having received the brunt of the fall, felt like someone struck it with a wooden bat. To her relief, the ground was heavily laden with trampled onychiopsis ferns that cushioned her fall. Without the extra safety net, she feared her shoulder may have become dislocated. Her legs were a different story; as Denny helped her to her feet, a sharp pain speared her in the knee. If they were fortunate enough to escape, she would need medical attention when they arrived in the twenty-second century.

"You okay, Lex'?"

"Just my knee," she waved him on. "Nevermind, worry later."

Denny pulled her sideways as the pair leaned on each other for support. The TimeGate stairwell loomed twenty yards ahead, accessible only from a single route through the maze of toppled tents and fallen hadrosaurs.

"This is incredible," Denny gawked, staring at the carnivores.

"Absolutely incredible," Alexis repeated, flipping open her viewfinder and hitting record.

In a fight over Manuel's remains, both tyrannosaurs— the only creatures left in the ruined base camp—commenced a herculean duel. In a deadly duet of slashing claws and chomping mouths, both carnivores traded blows, making the walk to the TimeGate a hazardous trek. To Alexis' horror, the red light over the portal rim began to flicker. A second later, the glass bulb burst within the cage, raining shards down on the platform.

The TimeGate was damaged beyond repair, struggling to retain control of Caruthers' assigned time-loop settings.

"Double time it, Alexis!"

"Right."

The pair accelerated their hobble, with what Alexis likened to a two-legged race when a pair of runners were tethered together. The first tyrannosaur delivered a swift bite to the back of the second dinosaur's shoulder girdle. Both combatants remained upright, fighting directly in front of the TimeGate on the steel steps.

"Oh God!" Denny uttered, lips quivering uncontrollably.

With both rexes occupying the majority of the access ramp, they would have to cut right through the climactic battle to escape.

Alexis hit pause on the camera, knowing the last few seconds would require her full attention.

And my ex thought I'd never accomplish anything, Alexis thought, hobbling toward danger.

The imagery was surreal. The second tyrannosaur finally broke free of the hold, ducking low and sinking a powerful bite on its rival's side. The maneuver prompted a sudden cyclonic maneuver from both creatures, as one sought escape whilst the other craved victory.

The platform rumbled as Denny led the way up the stairs. Alexis watched the TimeGate wobble by the thunderous footfalls of the warring tyrants, praying the time-loop would sustain itself.

"*Heads up,* kid!"

In a flash, the two groups converged.

Being within the tumultuous dinosaurs was akin to passing through the eye of a hurricane. Scaly reptilian legs stomped and pounded, while sharp claws flashed like katana blades. Shadows flooded both humans as the torsos of the tyrannosaurs blocked out the sun. Denny yelped, receiving a laceration to his arm courtesy of an ankle-mounted dewclaw. In the eye of the storm, Alexis caught the eye of the first tyrannosaur as it turned away from its attacker.

"Shit!"

The animal opened its jaws wide, anticipating both humans to fall right into its gullet.

Alexis screamed involuntarily, unable to prevent her demise as she faced oncoming death. Denny screamed louder, the closer of the pair to the carnivore's gaping maw.

In a flash, the second tyrannosaur flung its opponent away down the steps. With a snap of its jaws, Alexis watched as the maw snap down, only inches above her face, before the creature soared overhead, tumbling violently down the TimeGate ramp. The second tyrannosaur, relishing in a moment of victory, watched both humans dart up the stairs. Anticipating her foot placement, Alexis locked eyes with the apex carnivore as it gazed down. To her relief, the rex turned, lumbering down the stairs to resume the fight.

"We made it!" Denny cried in relief, practically leaping into the dying wormhole.

Particles ate away at his denim jacket and baseball cap. His body was rendered to tiny bits of information that transcoded his intelligence, likeliness, and consciousness. In a second he was gone, to a plane where where time and space melded.

Alexis reached the portal rim, looking back at the utter carnage wrought by the tyrannical duo. Both rexes had taken positions at the base of the TimeGate platform, initiating round two of their primal brawl. The base camp had been rendered to shredded tarps and faulty equipment. Two billowy smoke trails graced the sky; one from a tent that previously housed electronics equipment, and the second from the toppled command center. Across the expanse, Alexis saw survivors of the hadrosaur herd regrouping, trotting along the Eastern edge of the prairie toward the flats.

Whoa!

The damage from the first tyrannosaur was taking hold of the TimeGate. With a flash, a torrent of sparks flew out from a junction box, sending flaming contrails cascading down the vehicle access side-ramp. Another blast ruptured atop the rim, frying circuitry. When a third wave of sparks dispersed from the opposite junction box, Alexis guessed the location might become permanently inaccessible.

She stepped backward, feeling her body being rendered into binary data as her right hand slipped through time. Knowing her operation may never return to this moment, she glimpsed one final look at the ruins of the base camp, noting the droves of victims, both human and dinosaur, deceased on the clearing.

As the portal whisked her away in time, she resolved to strongly voice her opinion when she returned. Her superiors would find it highly controversial, she knew, and her termination would be imminent.

The Cretaceous Initiative would need shut-down immediately, until more proper security measures were put in place.

With that, her body was whisked away, watching as the two tyrannosaurs destroyed the remainder of the camp, vying for the title of tyrant of the valley.

THE END

Please consider learning an honest review of this book online.

Reviews help authors get noticed.

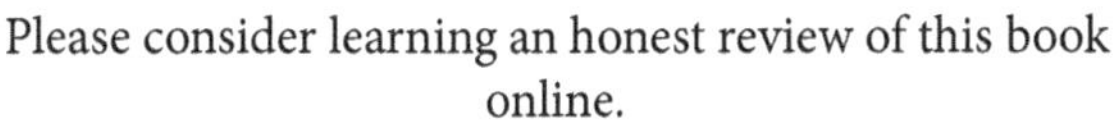

Thank you.

Julian Michael Carver

ABOUT THE AUTHOR

Joey Kelly (known by his pen name Julian Michael Carver) was born in Pittsburgh in 1992. He graduated from the now defunct Art Institute of Pittsburgh in 2013 with a degree in Visual Effects and Motion Graphics. In addition to writing, Carver is employed as a commercial editor. He uses his skills in multimedia to help market his books. In addition to commercial design work, Carver is also an avid fossil hunter. Carver currently lives north of Pittsburgh with his wife, Cloey. In 2022, his novelization of the film *Freshwater* was nominated for the Scribe Award by the international Association of Media Tie-in Writers.